Re
# THE DARK ATTIC

"Standing like a tree, hands like clouds, yielding and redirecting . . . *The Dark Attic* by Voychehovski and Prater is an adventure story wrapped in lessons from Tai Ji. Alex has lost his mother. Stephen is in a wheelchair. Sophia gets into the wrong crowd. Guided by Tai Ji lessons with Dr. Bingze, a mysterious computer game, and a magic book where pictures fly off the page, they learn to find strength in their weaknesses and, ultimately, the rewards of friendship. Anyone studying martial arts or interested in Eastern philosophy will want to read this book."

—Eleanor McCallie Cooper, author of *Dragonfly Dreams* and *Grace in China*

"*The Dark Attic* is amazing. First, it is a story that invites readers to its world of young people with its friendships, conflicts, problems, and secrets. It is also showing how to talk to young people about the mysterious and powerful art of Tai Ji. It teaches how one can find incredible adventure and magic. Without a doubt, many girls and boys will be attracted to Tai Ji practice after reading this book. What is even more important—they may become people you want to meet."

—Piotr Wojciechowski, eighty-four years old, philosopher, poet, author of books for children and adults, and Tai Ji practitioner in Warsaw, Poland

"Readers will be drawn into this fast-paced adventure that delivers a suspenseful read full of mystery, magic, and friendship."

—Betty Fudge, award-winning author of *Norm and Ginger Enter the Hidden*

"*The Dark Attic* is a highly entertaining novel for readers of all ages, even those of us who are young at heart yet long in the tooth! It is a literal page-turner, keeping the reader on edge, waiting for the next adventure in both the real world of the characters and the magical world of Tai Chi. Children will be enthralled, even as they are taught philosophical questioning and tolerance interlaced into the narrative. The strong moral code of the story will please parents as it encourages children to begin to look past superficial distractions and strive for purpose and meaning in their lives. I cannot wait for the next adventures of Alex, Stephen, and Sophia!"

—Michael Charles, author of *Bob and the Afterland*.

"*The Dark Attic* mixes a perfect blend of futuristic technology and pure magic to send readers on an adventure through a legendary ancient world. Young readers will be drawn to the cast of endearing characters with relatable tween issues and will cheer Stephen and Alex on as they explore their own strengths and weaknesses, the enchanting art of Tai Chi, and the overwhelming power of true friendship. Beautifully written and sure to entertain!"

—Susan Diamond Riley, award-winning author of *The Sea Witch's Revenge*, *The Sea Turtle's Curse*, and *The Sea Island's Secret*

"The fundamentals of Tai Chi philosophy are woven effortlessly throughout this fantastical tale of adventure and self-discovery! Readers of all ages will find themselves immersed and excited to turn the next page!"

—Beth Herring, Tai Chi student and instructor

"This book has a lot of figurative language, and I like the future 2067 concept with all the robots and more developed technology. I also liked the plot and all the details."

—Alicia Guo, age eleven

"I like using virtual reality for an ancient Chinese tradition like Tai Ji. I think Alex is a very disciplined and smart guy for avoiding fights and being friends with someone everyone thinks of as a loser."

—Alex Guo, age thirteen

"Personally, I enjoy this book. It has excitement while also explaining a martial art. The Grand Canyon was my favorite part because of how I could visualize the event aslmost perfectly, and it was so exciting."

—Lea Kunesh Kurtz, age eleven

*The Dark Attic*
*A Tai Ji Tale*

by Tom Voychehovski and Lucas Prater

© Copyright 2022 Tom Voychehovski and Lucas Prater

Illustrations by Dosia Boroń

ISBN 978-1-64663-826-0

Published by

3705 Shore Drive
Virginia Beach, VA 23455
800-435-4811
www.koehlerbooks.com

# THE
# DARK
# ATTIC

*A Tai Ji Tale*

## TOM VOYCHEHOVSKI
## *and* LUCAS PRATER

Illustrations by Dosia Boroń

VIRGINIA BEACH
CAPE CHARLES

*A special thank you to Dr. Zibin Guo for his teaching and inspiration. He has created a unique program, Applied Tai Ji, which makes Tai Ji accessible to people of all abilities. Find out more at appliedtaiji.com.*

*This book is dedicated to all wheelchair practitioners of Tai Ji.*

# Table of Contents

# *A Note*

Tai Ji is as much a philosophy as a martial art and as much a meditation as an exercise. It takes a good teacher and a lot of practice to get good at it, but the rewards are many: better focus, a calmer mind, and improved physical balance. It benefits people of all ages.

# CHAPTER 1

## *New York*

Alex and his father usually stayed in a hotel or a bed-and-breakfast place. Alex preferred hotels. In hotels, he felt like he was part of a detective story. He loved to hang out in the lobby and watch all the strangers coming and going, riding elevators up and down. He would make up stories for each one, imagining that they were spies or superheroes or Martians in disguise. He spent hours exploring long corridors and flexing his imagination. Sometimes, he found another "hotel kid" he could join forces with. And, of course, he could order cheeseburgers and fries from room service.

Bed-and-breakfasts were a different story. In the bed-and-breakfast places, he always had to sit up straight and carry on conversations with boring old ladies who pinched his cheeks or patted his head and asked him questions like "How old are you? Twelve? So big!" and "What's your favorite school subject? Recess? Hahaha!"

*Ugh,* he would think to himself. *Middle schools don't even have recess!*

But this time, it was different. Alex and his dad were going to stay where his dad grew up—New York City! The setting for movies. The city that never sleeps. The Big Apple!

It was early March and the sky over New York was low and gray when they stepped off the plane. An auto-cab took them to Brooklyn, where they got dropped off in front of one of the many townhouses on one of the many dark, tree-lined streets in the Chinese part of town. Alex jumped out of the cab onto the wet curb and immediately pulled his hoodie over his head. He shook his arms out and adjusted the watch-mii on his wrist before stuffing his hands into his hoodie pockets. The air was chilly, and the rain wasn't making things any better. He toed a waterlogged earthworm that had squirmed its way up onto the sidewalk. His overactive imagination took him into the earthworm's subterranean world. He envisioned his way through the tunnels that the worm spent its life wriggling through—until the rain forced it to surface for air.

A truck rumbled down the street, and Alex snapped back to the present. He squinted as he looked up from under his hood at the townhouse that would be his new home. "Yuck," he muttered. "This place is ancient."

It took his father forever to appear on the other side of the auto-cab. Although he was on the short side, Dr. Lasko moved with the surety and grace of an athlete. He had green eyes and wavy, light brown hair that turned blond when he spent a lot of time in the sun. Alex didn't look like his father at all. His black hair was straight, and his brown eyes turned up at the ends. Alex's memories of his mother were fading after all these years, even if he was still thinking about her, but he knew he looked like her because of the little photograph his father carried in his billfold.

Dr. Lasko waved his wrist phone across the machine and paid

the fare. The auto-cab buzzed off, the sizzle of its tires on the wet blacktop fading as it sped away.

Alex's dad joined him on the sidewalk. "This is it." He patted Alex on the back. "It feels strange but sweet. It's almost been fifteen years."

Alex was only twelve, so he had never seen the townhouse before. To him, it didn't feel sweet at all. The place looked dreary, the windows dark and empty. No one had lived in the building for over a year, so it seemed hunched over with loneliness. The fact that it was late afternoon and already getting dark did nothing to help his impression. The front door didn't even have a normal lock—just an old, weathered brass deadbolt.

As his father fumbled through his pocket for the key, Alex scoffed. "No voice ID locks? This is 2067, not 1967!"

His dad grinned. "Nope! Just a tried-and-true classic." Alex's dad liked oldfangled things. Alex didn't get it. The lock stuck, of course. His father kept jiggling the key.

"Just needs a little grease," Dr. Lasko grumbled.

The rain poured down in sheets as Alex's father tried to get the clunky old lock to open. When he finally did, they hurried inside, dripping puddles in the foyer. They put down their luggage and went into the living room. Alex's heart sank.

Just brick and mortar and wood, this place was *really* old-fashioned. There were no modern creature comforts—no bio-sensing lights, no smart appliances, no central computer. The doorways were trimmed in wood that was the same coffee color as the floors. The furniture was covered in white sheets to keep off the dust, which made Alex think of ghosts lurking in the dark. Alex hated the dark. He always had.

His father grabbed some bags and headed to the stairs. "Let's get you settled first. You can have my old room in the attic!"

"What?" Alex was spacing out again, looking at the sad, cold living room. The fireplace was sadder and colder than everything else. Above the mantle, there was a stone wall with a dark rectangle the sun hadn't reached. It looked like a picture had been hung there.

"Dad, was there a painting there?" Alex was pointing at the fireplace. "What was it of?"

"The painting, ah . . . the painting?" Alex looked at his father. Something was wrong. Dad's happy mood was gone, his mouth twisted. Was he going to cry?

"It was a picture of her," he almost whispered. "Your mother." Alex did not say anything. Nobody moved. Alex knew that his father was a strange man with heavy secrets. Maybe it was why he loved him so much? He was not going to hurt the old man, no matter what. As curious as he was about his mother, he dropped the subject.

At last, Alex's father started up the stairs. Alex slipped his backpack on and followed, grabbing the banister to steady himself. They went up two flights to the attic. His father felt around the wall by the door and flicked on the ceiling lights. One of the glass bulbs flickered. Alex peered anxiously around the room. It had a high, A-frame ceiling, a triangular window near the top of the far wall, and a triangular, floor-to-ceiling bookshelf built into the corner.

"This was my room when I was growing up. Now it's yours. You're going to love it here, buddy." His father walked across the room and tightened the flickering bulb, which suddenly shone solidly like the others. He grinned and tousled Alex's hair. "Wipe up all the dust and settle in, okay? I'll bring you some sheets. Brush your teeth and get ready for bed when you're done. We need to have an early night." Dr. Lasko vanished down the stairs.

Alex looked around, gripped by unease. The lights were weak and high and did not reach the back half of the room, which was enveloped in darkness. A car drove by, its high beams flashing through the window and sending spidery shadows up the walls and onto the ceiling. As soon as the car was gone, the end of the room fell into darkness once more. Alex realized that he didn't have a flashlight; his wristwatch was charging. He froze.

The dark.

He gulped. His mind raced through all the creepers and ghouls that could be watching him from the cracks in the far wall. A vampire? A space alien? Some weirdo goblin thing he didn't even know about yet? The more he looked, the more his bedroom seemed like the set of a horror movie. For crying out loud, this house was even older than his dad. It was probably haunted, and now he, Alex Lasko, was about to meet an untimely end in its ghastly abyss.

Alex noticed a second switch. It was right next to the one his father had flicked on. A light for the far wall? He didn't move, his eyes flitting between the switch and the darkness at the other end of the room. Some primal part of his brain told him to remain completely still. If he moved toward the switch, something would jump out and grab him. His heart was beating out of his chest. His dad thought he had gotten over his fear of the dark years ago because Alex had stopped calling for help like a baby. Slowly, he worked up his courage. *Spooks flee from light,* he reasoned. *They hate light as much as I hate the dark!* He made a mad dash for the switch. Adrenalin shot through him, and he let out a gasp.

# CHAPTER 2

## *A Surprise*

Click!

Alex turned, shaking and wide-eyed as a single light bulb at the end of the room came on, revealing . . . an empty wall. He caught his breath, feeling sheepish. He'd let his imagination get the better of him again. There was nothing in the room except a spindly iron bedstead, a long narrow desk, and a chair. Now that the room was lit up, it was a bit cozier, like a sleeping loft in a winter cabin.

Now, what had his dad told him to do? Alex groaned as he remembered. He hated dusting—and this room was covered with it. Cobwebs had accumulated in every nook and cranny. He didn't have a duster, but growing up on the road had made him self-sufficient. He pulled an old T-shirt out of his backpack and wiped off the desk and chair. When he got to the bookshelf, he swiped off each shelf, starting with the bottom. When he got about halfway up, he realized he would have to stand on the chair to reach the top two shelves.

He slid the chair over and hopped up. Something was strange. The paneling at the back of the top shelf didn't match the rest of the wall. *Weird,* he thought. He inspected the panel. There was a tiny hole about the size of a penny in the corner. He peered at the hole and knocked on the wall. It sounded hollow. He paused; then he wrapped his hand in the now dusty, wadded-up shirt, reached up, stuck his thumb in the hole, and slid the panel back.

"A secret hiding spot! Cool!"

Was there anything in it? It was dark inside, but he could just barely make out a shape near the back corner. "What is it?" he asked out loud. "A huge spider? A box? A dead rat? This is nuts—I can't just go shoving my hands into dark holes!"

But he was curious. He banged on the wood, but nothing moved. He could see well enough to tell that there weren't any spiderwebs inside, so he decided to chance it. He stood on his tiptoes as he reached his whole arm in. Even so, he could barely reach the thing. *A little deeper*, he thought. He felt the roughness of the wall plaster. He stuck his tongue out in concentration and stretched his arm as far as he could. His fingertips brushed against something.

It snapped into his grasp, and his hand tingled.

"Whoa!" he said. He pulled his arm out of the hiding place and looked at his prize. It was a book, colorful and thin, just three folded panels. It looked old, it felt old, and it smelled old—ancient, maybe by a hundred years, even! It was covered in beautiful paintings of mountains and animals. His hand was still tingling from whatever it was that had made the book jump into his grasp.

Carefully holding the slim volume, he got down from the chair and sat on the bed. Somehow, he was more careful than usual. He startled when the old box springs creaked under his weight. He wiped his hands on his shirt. Holding the book lightly with his fingertips, he opened the panels. The words inside were written in graceful Chinese calligraphy. He could not read any of them, but as he scanned the page, the characters morphed into English words. Amazed, he read the story out loud.

> *Stand like a tree, move like water. Far away in the tall Jade Mountains, there lived a beautiful princess named Ling.*

*Oh brother,* Alex thought. *A princess. Why couldn't I find a book about action heroes?* But he read on, astonished by the Chinese characters changing into English words.

> *Princess Ling roamed the forests and valleys on her horse, but she never hunted the animals. Instead, she painted them in the most magical way: they looked so alive, people swore they could see them move across the page.*
> *The cruel King Ka wanted to marry Princess Ling, but she did not love him, so she refused his proposal and ran away. King Ka sent his soldiers to capture her. They rode swift horses and caught up with her at the foot of the White Dragon Mountain.*
> *Great Crane, a good magician, was flying by. He saw what was happening, so to save her from the evil king, he turned the princess into a little spruce tree. The animals loved Ling and protected her. She grew straight and proud by a tumbling stream. Her roots spread into the earth, and she got taller and taller, as if reaching for the sky.*

Alex jumped off the bed, slamming the book shut. The stream had actually flowed across the page. The tree had swayed in the breeze. He had never seen digital tablets or e-paper like this! He shook his head. He had been trying to act more mature lately, but now he was imagining things like a little kid. Chinese writing did *not* morph into English. Pictures in books did *not* come alive.

Despite his misgivings, he cracked the book open and cautiously peered in. Good. Everything was still. He sat back down and opened the pages, admiring the illustrations.

*One spring day, a monkey was playing with the big rock on the top of White Dragon Mountain. He danced and pushed until it tipped over. Down it flew, gathering speed as it went.*

Alex watched as the boulder rolled down the steep slope, heading straight for the little spruce.

*The tiger, always alert, saw the danger and roared.*

Alex saw the beast as if it were in his room. Then a big panda leapt out of the forest and barreled across the page, his movements swishing through the watercolor landscape.

*The panda bear lunged and caught the boulder. He bent under its great weight, pushed the boulder sideways, and saved the princess.*

Alex was so caught up in the story, he couldn't take his eyes off the pictures moving across the page—the monkey's carefree dancing, the boulder crashing down the mountain, the tiger roaring, the panda lunging, the boulder rolling harmlessly away.

The story abruptly ended.

"Hot Helga," Alex said. He was proud of his new swear words. He had invented them a couple of weeks ago, after he'd broken the old Polaroid camera his father gave him to document their travels.

"So, what happens? If the crane crashes, the princess will always be a tree." He was about to close the book, but an inscription on the inside panel caught his eye.

*Remember, children. Play like the monkey, but watch what you're doing! Be alert like the tiger so you'll know what's going on around you. Use your strength like the panda bear, to help others.*

Alex groaned and fell back on the bed. "Sounds like my dad—especially the 'watch what you're doing' part." He decided he didn't like the book. The pictures were too real, the inscription was stupid, and he didn't even get to see how the story turned out. "It would be so much better if the princess had some kind of superpower, like Wonder Woman. Then she could fight the bad king herself."

He tossed the book onto the bed next to him.

He felt tired after a big day of airports and flights and taxis and new cities and moving into a new house. He let out a big yawn. *I'd better go to sleep,* he thought, *because tomorrow—Hot Helga!—tomorrow's the first day at my new school!*

Alex's father stuck his head through the door and tossed a set of sheets and a blanket on the newly dusted desk. "Here's some fresh linens. Have you brushed your teeth?"

"I forgot," Alex grumbled. *Brushing teeth,* he thought, *yet another chore to make me miserable.* He rolled his eyes and fell back on the bed to pout. A cloud of dust puffed out of the mattress. He started to cough wildly, pretending to have an asthma attack.

His father raised an eyebrow and shook his head. "Alex—teeth. *Now.*"

Alex sat up. "Dad, I found a really strange book in your secret hiding place."

His father was preoccupied with his watch-mii screen. Without looking up, he said, "Get ready for bed, buddy. Tomorrow's a big day!" He went back downstairs, where Alex could hear him talking on the phone.

"I guess I'll ask him about it later," Alex sighed.

He hopped down the rest of the stairs to the bathroom. The tiny, hexagonal tiles of the floor were cold on his feet. He squirted a glob of glittery toothpaste onto his toothbrush and pretended it was a samurai sword. He shook back his straight, black hair, squinted his dark, almond-shaped eyes, and made an intimidating ninja face at the bathroom mirror. "You must defend your honor!" he said in his best warrior voice. Then he thrust the sword forward in a surprise attack, smearing the toothpaste all over the mirror.

"Yarrrgh! Surrender!"

# CHAPTER 3

## *Another New School*

The next day, Dr. Lasko sat in the waiting room outside the principal's office at Brooklyn Central Middle School. The walls were plastered with posters about things like "Vision," "Excellence," and "Purpose." Dr. Lasko had to go through the song and dance of meeting the principal and teachers and explaining Alex's problems each time they moved to a new city. He was worried about his son.

The principal's assistant looked up from filing her nails. "Mr. Skeeter will see you now." Dr. Lasko got up. *Strange,* he thought, *how even now, I feel like I'm in trouble whenever I walk into the principal's office.* He grinned slightly to himself as he shook Principal Skeeter's hand.

Mr. Skeeter tapped the glass screen on his desk. "So, tell me about Alex. His file says that he's gotten into a bit of trouble over the years."

*Nothing like a nice, easy start,* Dr. Lasko thought. He cleared his throat to speak. "Alex is a smart, talented boy, but he can be careless."

"I see he has attention deficit. We can handle that."

"I don't like putting labels on kids."

"It's not a big deal," the principal said. "A lot of kids have it. But this business about getting into fights . . . Dr. Lasko, I don't mean to sound harsh, but here at Brooklyn Central, we set a high standard of behavior for our student body." Mr. Skeeter tapped his pen on his desk. "From what I've read in his file, Alexander seems to have anger issues. We simply don't tolerate fights."

Dr. Lasko shook his head. "Now let's not jump to extremes. I'd like you to know that there's just the two of us, and we've moved around a lot. I supply herbs and other ingredients to Chinese doctors who make specialized medicines for their patients."

Mr. Skeeter raised an eyebrow.

Dr. Lasko continued. "Alex has had to adapt to new classmates twice, sometimes three times a year. That can be difficult for a kid."

"Ah," Mr. Skeeter said. "And his mother?"

Dr. Lasko frowned. "She's gone." The downward pull of his face made him look ten years older.

"Are you separated, or did she pass away?" Mr. Skeeter asked.

"She's just gone. Let's leave it at that." Dr. Lasko shifted uncomfortably in his seat, but he firmly met the principal's eye.

Mr. Skeeter glanced at his watch and stood up. "I'm afraid my next meeting is about to begin. We'll give Alex all the support we can, but we'll keep a close eye on him. We'll be in touch should anything come up."

The two men shook hands again, and Dr. Lasko left the office, rolling his eyes. *Well, that went well,* he thought sarcastically. *I hope I don't have to come back here again.*

Alex was like his father's sidekick. Together they traveled all over the globe: Africa, Australia, and South America. Last year, they went to Latvia to obtain rare buckwheat honey for some ancient cough remedy. Alex loathed European schools, where new laws forbade computers in the classroom, instead opting for the traditional "chalk and blackboard" teaching method. They didn't even allow smart watches! So far, they had lived in Europe twice during Alex's twelve years, and he had treated it like punishment both times.

So, in the old, sprawling Brooklyn Central Middle School, he felt like a pro. A new school. A piece of cake. Being the "new boy" was a great excuse to be spaced out and slightly behind on his homework, but Alex prided himself on making friends and becoming popular. He made a game out of it. His newness would eventually wear off, but for a few weeks, he would be the center of attention, a shiny new toy for his classmates. Alex always loved this part. Everyone would be talking to him and asking him questions. He could say anything, be anybody. Even so, he told the truth—mostly.

"Oh yeah! My dad's a famous doctor in China. Sure! I've lived there. France? Absolutely! England? Definitely! Brazil? Twice!"

Before the morning was over, he found himself talking to a guy named John Novelli. John was very cool, very rich, and very popular. He had thick dark hair, wore a gold chain around his neck, and dressed in a shiny gray suit. Alex thought this was a little odd, but he went with it. John spoke with a loud, exaggerated Italian accent, sprinkling his speech with Italian words. He talked to everyone, including a girl named Sophia. John spoke to Sophia much too often, if you asked Alex. Was he her boyfriend? Alex had pinpointed the popular group, but he was still working out the relationships between all the kids in it.

Alex stole a glance at Sophia from across their circle. Her round blue eyes shined as she talked to her friends. Her hair fell in long, reddish-blond curls that bounced when she laughed. Alex was thinking about what he would say to her if and when he got the chance, but John nudged him, and he was jerked out of his daydream.

"*Buongiorno*! Hey, new boy! Alex, is it?" John's voice boomed like that of a benevolent king. "Tomorrow after school we're going to pick teams. Teams, *capiche*? Serious *gamola*. So, can the new boy play?"

Alex knew that John meant video games. Alex preferred lone wolf, quest-style games. He also liked RPGs—role-playing games—that he could play by himself. He tried to sound cool, though. "I play Around the World, Level Six, and sometimes Gamer R, arena style."

"Level Six?" John was not impressed. "I'm a level eight, bambino. As for GR, I'll have to show you my portable R sometime." He smacked Alex on the back. Then, turning to his plump sidekick, he said, "I'm hungry, Roger. I want a spicy *meat-a-bolla*!" Roger stared blankly at him through his shaggy bangs. Then he glanced dully at Alex, and he and John strutted off to find a snack. "Tomorrow, new boy!" John boomed over his shoulder. "We're gonna see if you've got skills!"

*I guess my audience with the king is over*, Alex thought. He let out a sigh and looked for Sophia, but she had disappeared down the hall. Classes hadn't started yet, so kids were milling around everywhere, playing handheld video games, typing on their watch-miis, playing hopscotch and foursquare, and laughing and talking with friends.

Alex smiled to himself. *This school's gonna be a cinch.*

# CHAPTER 4

## *Stephen*

The last class before lunch was computer science. Alex loved computer science. He was good at it, and he liked to show off, but when he arrived, he was momentarily intimidated. The class was held in the old gymnasium, which had been retrofitted with state-of-the-art robotics, electronics, computers, and other tech hardware. Crowds of students stood around in cliques, racing remote-control cars, battling remote-control robots, playing video games, and generally one-upping each other.

"Impressive," he acknowledged with a small nod.

He wandered through the room until he recognized some kids from his first-period class and trod over to join them. He was greeted mildly with "Hey, new kid, what's up?"

When the teacher walked in and announced the assignment, some of the students groaned, but Alex's confidence shot up a bit. Today's lesson was right up his alley: to program the class's humanoid robot to dance to a segment of "Beat It"—one of Michael Jackson's classic oldies. Alex had picked up a few tricks while moving from school to school all over the world. The Asian schools in particular had bolstered his programming skills. His natural interest in the subject didn't hurt either.

Alex's father called robots "overgrown appliances." They were definitely a big part of everyday life in 2067. They served burgers, picked up trash, and helped little kids and old people cross the street. The families who could afford it even had robotic maids and butlers that cooked, cleaned, and did the laundry. So, it was a given that basic knowledge about programming robots was an indispensable part of education.

The students were given half an hour to write their dance programs, after which they would make presentations. One of the walls of the old gymnasium was lined with a countertop that had programming terminals mounted to it. Each student took one of the terminals and before long, the *rat-a-tat* of computer keys filled the room as the kids typed out their dance sequences.

As the other students made the robot dance, Alex was glad to see that none of their programs were up to his standards. His was simple but creative. All he had to do was press "Enter" on his screen, and the monkey-sized robot would sway from side to side, then spin twice and finish by balancing on one foot and throwing its arms in the air. That was it. Classic. Several of his classmates laughed and clapped in appreciation. Most of them had only managed to make the robot move one of its arms or turn its head from side to side. He was beaming—until he saw the next presentation.

As the class watched, the robot swayed back and forth to the beat. Suddenly, its legs sprung apart, and then they quickly crisscrossed. Its arms flowed out like a wave. It moved its arms and legs rhythmically like a hip-hop dancer, tapping its feet heel to toe, rotating its arms and wrists, and spinning around like a dervish. It finished by going down into a split and popping back up into a spin, finally stopping with its arms crossed. The class erupted in applause.

Peeved, Alex turned his head, his mouth agape, looking for the student who had bested him. Stephen, a skinny kid with a big poof of curly red hair, was grinning from ear to ear, basking in his classmates' short-lived admiration.

*He would be tall if he could walk*, Alex thought. Stephen sat in a wheelchair, but not just any wheelchair. There was a computer built into it that Stephen spoke through. It was a voice synthesizer, which sounded a bit like a robot. Alex idly wondered if Stephen was part-robot, but the ridiculous thought left as quickly as it had come. Stephen's eyes met Alex's, and when they did, Stephen's mouth widened into a big, goofy grin. The grin was infectious, and Alex smiled back. Alex liked him from the moment he saw him. With that smile, Alex's envy melted away, and he knew he wanted to be friends.

When the bell rang and class broke for lunch, the hall was flooded with kids who scattered like marbles tossed on the floor. Alex got lost in the rush and ended up completely turned around. He never listened very well, especially when instructions were being given, so he had no idea how to navigate his new surroundings. He dashed around the emptying halls until he found the cafeteria. By then, it looked like everyone was already halfway through lunch. Catching his breath, he adjusted his shirt as he entered, trying to look cool. But his bravado quickly wilted before all his seated classmates, and something like stage fright set in as he walked across the crowded room. Alex got his food and looked for a place to sit, but the tables were full. Then he saw Stephen sitting alone. Alex sat down across from him, still catching his breath. Stephen smiled. "Hi. I'm Stephen." His voice sounded mechanical as he spoke through his synthesizer.

"I'm Alex. Hey, you really got that robot to dance."

"Your dance wasn't so shabby, either."

They ate and talked. The dull, computer-generated sound of Stephen's voice made the conversation bumpy at first, but Alex had listened to so many languages in his travels around the world that he quickly got used to it. The boys talked about creating new programs that could connect home appliances in crazy ways. The *internet of things*, the fact that most devices could talk to each other, was one of Alex's favorite topics.

"What if your freezer could connect to your neighborhood ice cream truck?" Alex asked. "It would be able to order Choco Tacos for breakfast every day!"

"Yes, and the ice cream trucks could detect low levels of ice cream in your freezer!" Stephen agreed.

"Ha ha! My dad would probably say that's a privacy issue!"

"That's a privacy I'd let go of. The ice cream truck should know when my freezer is low on ice cream. Duh!"

Time flew. Before they knew it, they were late for their next class.

Alex took their trays to the dishwasher robot. It scanned his face and mechanically said, "Thank you, young man."

When they finally walked into class, Stephen said, "I'm sorry we are late, Mr. Stosur. My wheelchair got stuck in the elevator and Alex unstuck me."

Their classmates snickered.

"Very well," Mr. Stosur said. "Next time, please get stuck before another teacher's class, okay?" But he smiled as they passed in front of him to take their places.

Alex looked over at Stephen and they grinned. During class, they snuck some instant messages to each other on their tablets. It was against the rules for students to pass instant messages during school hours, but Stephen had figured out a way to get around it.

Stephen: "I want to show you something cool. Can you hang out after school?"

Alex: "Absolutely, for sure!"

Stephen: "Okay, meet me out front after your last class!"

When the bell rang, Alex and Stephen parted ways. Alex had Literature and Stephen had American History. They confirmed their plans to hang out after school, bumped fists, and then Stephen rolled his wheelchair down the hall in the opposite direction. When Stephen had made it about halfway down the hall, some other kids started snickering, and Alex heard one of them say, "Did you see that nerd-asaurus today in Computer Science?"

"Yeah, an ultra-weirdo!"

Alex frowned. He had clicked with Stephen so immediately that he hadn't stopped to consider what others thought about him. He'd also never been at a school with a wheelchair kid. Alex realized that Stephen was probably an outsider. Would it be social suicide to become friends?

# CHAPTER 5

## *Problems with Friends and Crows*

When school let out, Stephen waited patiently by the front entryway, but Alex did not show up. Dejected but not surprised, Stephen slowly wheeled himself across campus. He hoped his new friend was talking to a teacher and would soon catch up.

Alex wasn't talking to a teacher; he was hiding in the bathroom. After a while, he felt silly standing around in the stall, so he went outside. As he crouched behind a school bus, he saw Stephen wheeling himself down Oak Street, looking over his shoulder every now and then. As much as Alex wanted the other boys to think he was cool, his face burned with shame.

He ran. "Stephen! I lost you somehow."

"Oh. Hey." Stephen grinned.

Alex laughed uneasily, not sure if Stephen had guessed that he had second thoughts about their friendship.

"I ride the bus when the weather is bad," Stephen said, "but on a nice day like this, I like to take my chair."

"You said you wanted to show me something cool."

"I want you to meet my crows."

"Your what?"

"My crows. Big black birds. Don't you know what crows are?"

"Of course, I do." Alex wondered what he had gotten himself into. "I've just never *met* any. They're kind of dark and creepy."

"They're incredibly smart. You'll see."

Alex turned away and rolled his eyes. Maybe he should have stayed in the bathroom, after all.

As the boys went down the street, Stephen thought about how he began training crows in the first place. Even he acknowledged that it was a strange hobby.

Four years earlier, Stephen and his mother had moved to a much smaller apartment in a much humbler neighborhood. The move was sudden, and Stephen did not want to go. His mother never told him why they had to move, but he knew it made her sad. She had to sell her car and get up every morning before dawn to catch a train to work. Stephen had had to adjust to a new school and lots of time alone.

When they lived in their old neighborhood, Stephen had a nanny, Ms. Laura, who picked him up after school. He liked Ms. Laura. She had taken care of him ever since he could remember, but he hadn't seen her since the move. Now he came home to an empty house.

He knew his mother worried about him being alone so much. Their new, smaller apartment was stuffy, so Stephen had taken to rolling himself out to the sidewalk in front of the building when he got home. He enjoyed watching the people and cars go by—especially the people. They were all so different—all with their own unique stories. He liked to try to deduce things about them based on their appearance, like Sherlock Holmes. His mom didn't like him being out on the street in their new neighborhood. She spent every evening searching the internet for "wheelchair-friendly" after-school programs, but she never found any. Stephen knew she wouldn't. The world wasn't designed for people in wheelchairs.

One afternoon, Stephen was out in front of their building people watching when three men passed by. They were all wearing black karate suits and carrying long bags, which looked like they contained weapons, maybe swords of some kind. The men looked super cool. Stephen wondered if they were samurais or kung fu monks. His interest piqued, and he rolled down the sidewalk after them.

They entered a mid-rise about two blocks away. The glass door was decorated with a big red Chinese character. Above it, the word *Wuguan* was printed in red letters.

Stephen scratched his head. He wanted to know what a *wuguan* was. He looked left. He looked right. Then he took a deep breath and went through the door into a small, drab lobby. It seemed like the only way to follow the men was to take the elevator. It was a large freight elevator with bars for doors. Stephen wrestled the doors open and got in. There were six buttons on the control panel and the one at the very bottom was marked *Taijiquan*. He pressed it. The elevator rattled as it lurched into motion, slowly taking him into the bowels of the building. He broke into a cold sweat. He calmed down by reminding himself that Sherlock Holmes was never scared, not even when he was following Moriarty.

The elevator landed with a clatter. Stephen wheeled himself into a long concrete hallway. Fluorescent tubes flickered their cold light onto the walls. At the end of the hall was a scratched metal door with a small window in it. Stephen couldn't see through the window, but above the door, he noticed a circular symbol—two interlocking swirls of white and black. He opened the door.

A group of men and women of all shapes, sizes, and colors were standing in rows, as still as statues. Each wore a karate suit that looked like black silk pajamas. As Stephen watched, transfixed, he realized that they weren't standing like statues at all. They were moving slowly and deliberately, pushing their hands this way and that as if moving some invisible force around the room. They moved in unison, stopping and starting as one unit. Stephen watched until they finished. The students scattered. Some people stood around talking to each other. Others headed out the door. Two of the women walked over to a bench near Stephen to rest and sip from their water bottles.

"What was that you were doing?" Stephen asked.

The women looked around for the source of the robotic voice. When their eyes landed on Stephen, they smiled, and one of them said, "Tai Ji!"

A short, muscular Chinese man walked over. "Greetings!" He gave Stephen a big toothy smile. "I am Dr. Bingze. This is my studio. Did you enjoy watching the class?"

"Yes," Stephen said excitedly. "I've never seen anything like this before. What's Tai Ji? Why was everybody moving their hands around? What's a *wuguan*—"

Dr. Bingze raised his hand. "All good questions, young man. And I will answer them. But first, we must be properly introduced. I've told you my name. What is yours?"

"Stephen, sir."

"Well, Stephen," Dr. Bingze said, looking intently into Stephen's eyes. "Tai Ji is an ancient martial art. It teaches us how to defeat our opponents by using their own power against them." He stretched out his arms, pointing at the walls of the room. "And this is a *wuguan*—a martial arts studio." He pulled a small slip of paper out of his pocket. "Give your parents my card. I would be pleased to see you in my next class."

That night, Stephen told his mother about his adventure. She chided him for following strange people into strange buildings, but she also wondered if Tai Ji classes would give Stephen something to do besides hang out on the sidewalk.

After dinner, Stephen went on the internet to find out more about this mysterious martial art. He read about ancient Tai Ji masters who studied animals. They watched their habits and movements and used what they saw in their practice. Stephen thought about what animals he could watch. The city didn't have very many tigers and monkeys, but it did have crows. So as time went by, he became a bit of an expert on them.

He might have preferred to hang out with a group of friends, but for now, the crows made him happy.

Stephen and Alex made their way through the neighborhood.

"I've been meaning to ask," Alex said, "why you never put your chair in auto mode."

"For exercise!" Stephen said. "My upper body is super strong."

As they trekked around the next corner, they came upon a park dotted with spreading hemlocks and tall tulip poplar trees. Alex sat on a bench surrounded by big rose bushes, and Stephen rolled up next to it. It was still cold, but spring was in the air. The grass and bushes were starting to turn green, and the crocuses added splashes of yellow and purple to the world again.

"Watch this," Stephen said. He cawed twice through his voice box. "*Crraaaw! Craaaw!*" A moment later, three crows circled over the boys and landed in front of the bench.

"Jack's the biggest, Jackie's the smallest, and Jackleen's the prettiest," Stephen announced, pointing to each. To Alex, they all looked the same.

"What do they do?" he asked.

"Mostly eat," Stephen said matter-of-factly. He pulled some bread out of the backpack that hung from his chair. "I'm teaching them to open the door with a key," he added, as if this was no big deal. He pointed to a shelf under his chair, which held two storage boxes with simple locks.

"No way! Can they do it?" Alex forgot about the weirdness of Stephen's hobby.

"Not exactly, not yet," Stephen admitted. "But they will. Crows are so smart—scientists call them feathered apes. Watch this."

Stephen unsnapped one of the boxes and began talking to the crows. "Okay, Jack, here's the food. I'm locking it in this box with a key. Alex will put the box on that bench over there with the key beside it. See?" He held the key up in front of the bird's shiny black eye, and then handed it over to Alex.

The two boys watched as the crows pranced and cawed with excitement. One of them picked the key up in its beak and tried to put it in the keyhole. It fell out.

"Good job, Jackleen! Here, let me show you," Stephen said. "This is how it's done."

He opened the box and let the crows peck happily at the bread.

"Want to try, Jack, you big boy?"

After about a half an hour of near-successes, Alex got cold and fidgety. "I've got to go. I have a lot of homework."

"Want to hang out tomorrow?"

"Sure thing. See you in class." Alex grinned over his shoulder. As he ran home, he thought about how strange his new friend was. He'd never met anyone like Stephen.

# CHAPTER 6

## *Sophia*

The next day, Alex didn't show up to help train the crows.
He planned to, but Sophia, along with John-the-Italian-King and a group of other laughing classmates, swept him into the game room.

He felt guilty for ignoring Stephen, but he was ecstatic to end up at a console with Sophia. Roger, who kept scratching his greasy hair with the controller, sat between them. Even though Roger was bulky, Alex felt lucky. In the game, at least, Roger wouldn't come between him and Sophia.

"Let's play Animal Royale," Sophia said. They had just played a round of Gamer R, and she had creamed both of them. Animal Royale was mostly popular with girls, but after the way she smiled . . . Roger and Alex couldn't say no. Roger grinned and shook his head at Alex in recognition of their shared plight. Sophia was clearly in charge here.

"I'll be the Elephant," she said. "How about you, new boy?"

"The Crow." Alex was startled by his own answer.

"The Crow? That's funny," Sophia laughed. "It's actually pretty great. No one ever picks it. Why did you?"

She looked at him with her round blue eyes, clearly interested in his answer. Was she flirting? Wasn't she going with John? She smiled—not at Roger and him, but at him alone. His stomach went fluttery.

"They're incredibly smart," Alex explained, parroting Stephen. "They can solve really complex problems."

Sophia kept looking at him, as if expecting more.

"And, umm, they're really fun to watch," he blurted out. *Fun to watch?* Alex mentally slapped his forehead.

"Well, let's watch them sometime," she said.

"Okay." With excitement and a touch of fear, he thought, *definitely flirting.*

Back home in his room, Alex plopped down on his bed and punched his pillow. How could he be friends with Stephen and not have everyone think he was a dweeb? He liked Stephen, but he'd ditched him so he could hang out with Sophia. His happiness at being with her was already fading. He was mad at himself. Actually, he was ashamed.

He paced around his room. He stood up on his bed and looked out the little triangular window. He had to stand on his tiptoes, and he couldn't really see anything anyway, so he plopped back down on the bed. He gazed across the room at his desk. On it, there was one object: the Chinese picture book he'd found hidden in the wall. Alex walked over to his desk and sat down. He thought about what he'd read a few days earlier—a weird story about a tree standing in a valley and a boulder rolling down the mountain toward it and a panda who jumped in to stop the boulder from crushing the tree.

Alex picked up the book. He felt the parchment in his hands. It was thick, grainy, and the color of oatmeal. *It's really old*, he thought. He noticed that the front cover in his left hand felt thicker than the back cover in his right. That was strange. Why would the front be thicker than the back? Was there another page hidden inside? He peered at the edge of the cover, gingerly picking at it with his fingernail. It suddenly came apart.

Alex gasped. There was indeed a secret panel—another moving panel—but it wasn't of an animal trying to rescue a silly tree. A Chinese girl was gracefully backing up and blocking an invisible opponent with her arms. Behind her, a family of monkeys laughed and jeered, slowly but rudely waving their arms. Suddenly, out of the blue, another, much bigger monkey leapt onto the page. The girl wobbled and was about to fall when Alex slammed the book face-down on his desk.

"Hot Helga, not again!" He jumped out of his chair. "I must be going crazy. It stops when you focus, it moves when you relax?" It did not feel like a supercomputer or hologram, it felt so ancient, so, so . . . magical? He paced the room, staring at the book. He sat back down at the desk. Squeezing his eyes shut, he turned the book over.

Nothing moved. The girl's arms stayed in the air, blocking her invisible opponent. The monkeys were frozen as they laughed and jeered. Nothing leaped onto the page.

> *If the girl wants to repel the monkey, she must keep her balance. She must stand like a tree.*

Alex sighed in relief. The girl was safe! Setting the book aside, he went downstairs to brush his teeth. It had been a strange day. First crows, now monkeys. Alex decided he preferred the crows.

"I am also going to stand like a tree," he told himself. "Tomorrow I'm going to tell Stephen I'm sorry. And one of these days, his crows are going to figure out how to use that key."

The next day at school, things were not so simple. Alex had planned to apologize to Stephen after his first class. After the bell rang, he went to the hall, spotting Stephen talking to a teacher. He started toward him but bumped into Sophia instead.

"Hi, crow guy." She smiled. "How are your feathers this morning?"

Before he could think of a witty answer, John walked up.

"Hey, hey! New kid! You showed a little skill the other day in the game room. Maybe there's hope for you yet! We are going to play TRIO at *mi casa* today after school. Serious game-peezy. Be there or be square! *Capiche*?"

TRIO was the newest 3D basketball game for the Z-Box gaming system. Players had to put on a virtual reality headset and jump around to play the game. It was like playing the real game except you could be any size or height you wanted and play in whatever city or location you wanted. You could even play on the moon!

"Uh . . ." Alex stammered. He wanted to apologize to Stephen, but all the cool kids were standing around him in a circle, waiting for him to accept John's invitation.

"Yeah! Awesome!" he blurted out.

"Cool! Meet us out front after school. You're going down, *amico mio*!" John pumped his fist in the air and turned to leave. As he did, his entourage followed him like puppies.

"*Arrivederci!*" he said to Alex, then to Sophia, "C'mon, *bella*."

Alex looked down the hall at Stephen, who was still talking to the teacher. Classes were changing and the hall was emptying fast. Alex sighed, thinking, *I'll apologize tomorrow, I guess.* He hurried down the hall to his class, hoping that Stephen hadn't seen him.

# CHAPTER 7

## *Standing Like a Tree*

After school, John yelled, "Come on!" A bunch of kids followed. Alex was about to join them when Stephen rolled up.

"Hey. Want to go to the park?" Stephen was grinning from ear to ear.

*He's not mad at me?* Alex thought with relief. *But what about John? I really want to play TRIO.* He picked up his backpack, avoiding Stephen's gaze. "Uh, yeah. About the park—I don't know. It's kind of cold."

Stephen's smile faded. Alex hated hurting his friend's feelings, but he really wanted to hang out with the popular kids. Uncertain, he glanced over at John, who was staring at him, his hands in his pockets and a scowl on his face.

*Beep beep beep.* The screen on Stephen's computer flashed as it beeped, lighting up to reveal the words: STANDING LIKE A TREE.

Words from the strange Chinese book—what were they doing on Stephen's computer? This could not be a coincidence. It was a mystery, maybe even magic! Alex took a deep breath, turned to John, and said, "Hey, man, something's come up. I'll have to catch you later. Raincheck?"

"Later?" John's face got red. He put his fists on his hips and tapped his toes. "So, you'd rather hang out with the cripple? What are you going to do? Push him around the park and feed the birds like a couple of grandpas?"

Alex felt the fury boil up inside his chest. He hadn't known Stephen long, but he wasn't going to stand for John disrespecting his friend. "Jerk!" Alex yelled. He made a fist and was lunging toward John when Stephen's computer screen beeped and flashed again: STANDING LIKE A TREE. Alex froze. "That Chinese story again? How come it's on—" He tripped over the footplate of Stephen's wheelchair. As he fell forward, his leg brushed Stephen's foot. And then, time stopped.

In front of him was John, paralyzed as he prepared to receive Alex's punch. The other kids, the cars, the birds—they all stopped in place. It seemed like the whole world was captured in a photograph, but was still alive and buzzing inside, trying to get out. Even the last, misty exhalation Alex had made was frozen in the air.

The colors of the world got brighter and more saturated, as if someone was turning a dial all the way up. He and Stephen stared in amazement, first at each other and then at Stephen's screen. It was beeping faster and faster and getting bigger and bigger. The world shattered into a million tiny cubes. Alex put his hand on Stephen's shoulder, and the boys whooshed into the screen. Alex felt like he was on a rollercoaster with stars rushing by, the roar of wind and water filling his ears.

Alex squeezed Stephen's shoulder. His head tingled, and he felt strangely connected, as if their two brains and the computer were merging into one. There was an enormous burst of light;

then everything went dark. From the silence, the sounds of a forest emerged—birds chirping and wind-rustling leaves. The air smelled fresh and cool. Alex felt warm sunlight on his face.

The darkness cleared. On a distant hill, Alex saw a little red and black temple. Its roof had upturned corners. The building looked familiar, like the ones he'd seen when he and his father were living in . . . he couldn't quite remember where. Then it came to him: China! *We can't be in China,* he thought.

Alex was in a lovely clearing in the middle of a mountain forest. Next to him stood a sapling, a little tree. He tried to move, but he couldn't, at least not in the way he was used to. Panic snaked up his stomach to his mind. This must be a new kind of immersive virtual reality, but it sure did feel like he was planted deep in the mud in the Chinese countryside.

Alex whispered, "Stephen?"

The sapling next to him whispered back, "Alex?"

Alex reached out to touch the little tree. Horrified, he saw that his own arm had turned into a branch and his fingers into leaves.

"*Aahgh*!" Alex screamed.

"Uh-oh!" Stephen said cheerfully. "We got sucked into my ASP."

Alex waved his leafy arms around. "What's an ASP?" he shouted. His branches creaked and his foliage rustled. "As soon as possible?"

"No, it's a new game they put on my computer when they repaired it last week," Stephen, (the sapling), explained. "ASP stands for Adventure Study Program. It's something my Tai Ji teacher invented. I'm helping him test it, but this is the first time it's ever worked!"

*I wish it hadn't,* Alex thought. *How will we ever get home?*

*I don't know,* Stephen answered.

They stared at each other in amazement. Neither one of them had spoken out loud, but it was as if they had. Apparently, they were reading each other's minds.

"This keeps getting weirder and weirder," Alex said. "You know what else? Your computer voice is gone."

"You're right!" Stephen said. "Wow. So, this is what I really sound like."

At that moment, dark, ominous clouds rolled in. The wind picked up, whipping the boy-trees wildly about and knocking them into each other.

"We have to get back!" Alex yelled through the howling wind. "And I don't see an escape button in the upper left corner of the sky!"

"All I know is, we have to learn something to get back. And if we don't learn it fast, the wind will pull us up by the roots!" Stephen shouted.

Thunder boomed, lightning flashed, the clouds ripped open, and rain poured down in sheets. Alex and Stephen could barely see each other.

*What do we have to learn?* Alex wondered.

*Something about Tai Ji,* Stephen answered. *I think Dr. Bingze wants us to know what it means to stand like a tree!*

Alex forgot that their brains were connected and yelled as loud as he could, "What's Tai Ji, and who is Doctor Biiiingzeeee?"

Stephen suddenly remembered what to do. "Okay! Listen up! It's just like Dr. Bingze says. Spine straight! Drop down! Feel your feet connect with the earth!"

Thunder boomed, followed by a lightning bolt that scorched the sky and hit an old, gnarled tree. Shards of wood went flying in every direction. Sparks sent blinding light into the black clouds, illuminating the forest and the clearing. A huge limb crashed down through the canopy, snapping branches as it went and landing with a sickening thud just inches from the boys.

Alex almost jumped out of his skin—rather, his bark. As he struggled to run away, he felt his roots loosen in the puddle at his feet. If he kept this up, he realized, he would fall facedown into the mud.

"Breathe in, all the way to your feet!" Stephen shouted. "Take root! Let your roots sink lower into the earth every time you breathe!"

Alex's limbs thrashed around in the howling wind. Just as he was about to fall over, Stephen reached out his arm. As the boys' branches touched, Dr. Bingze's teaching flowed directly from Stephen to Alex. Alex felt his breathing slow down. His feet sank deeper into the earth. His roots held.

The thunder rumbled over the mountains. The rain dwindled to a sprinkle and then to nothing at all. Birds chirped and the sun came back out.

"Wow." Stephen smiled. "So that's what it means to stand like a tree."

*But we're still trees,* Alex thought.

Stephen scratched his head, which looked funny since he didn't really have a head.

Alex laughed, and Stephen joined in. They wiggled their trunks. Alex was surprised at how much fun being a tree could be. "We're doing the tree shuffle hustle!" he said.

"Haha! We're all bark and no bite!" Stephen chimed in.

Alex suddenly recalled what had been happening right before he became a tree. John had insulted Stephen, which made Alex so mad he went after John, his fists flying. How dumb. What had made him think that breaking John's nose would help Stephen feel better? The problem, Alex realized, was that he *hadn't* been thinking. At that moment, he decided he would never fight John. *In fact,* he promised himself, *I'll never get sucked into a fight again.* He inhaled deeply, and the mountain landscape faded, melting into the fog.

Alex and Stephen were back at school. Alex was charging toward John with clenched fists, but right before smashing John's nose, Alex pivoted. Stumbling, he almost fell, but he found his balance and walked away. *Hot Helga!* he thought. *Stephen's game must have liked my decision not to get sucked into another fight. It brought us right back!*

# CHAPTER 8

## *Fight/No Fight*

"What happened?" John sneered. "Chicken out?"

"Let's have a TRIO match some other time." Alex was surprised by how calm he sounded. "Stephen and I already had plans."

John stood there, his face turning red. He looked at his friends. They shrugged. "Noooo, no, new kid. You cancel on me, there *is* no other time. *Capiche*?" He got within inches of Alex's face. "I hope you and your robot pal here are happy together because you'll never hang with us again. You're out." He pushed Alex. All the other kids, Stephen included, gasped. Alex itched to push John back, or better yet, finish the punch he had started before getting sucked into the ASP. But he held firm. As he controlled his anger, he felt stronger and stronger. Rooted, like a great tree.

"I'm not going to fight you," Alex said.

"Fine, you wuss!" John huffed and sputtered. Sweat ran down his face even though it was cold.

Now that he was calm, Alex felt like an observer, as if he were watching the situation unfold on television. The more worked up

John got, the more ridiculous he looked, like a toddler throwing a tantrum. Alex wished Sophia were there so she could see what a loser John was.

"Don't think for one minute that you're cool, new boy. C'mon!" John stalked off, and his friends followed. Alex's head was spinning. Stephen felt the same. It had all happened so fast, but now everything was back to normal. They could hardly wait to talk about the fight that didn't happen and the trip they had just had.

Stephen spoke first. "That was rotten luck. I get rid of my wheelchair, but I'm a tree rooted to the spot." He looked up at Alex. "Maybe that *was* the lesson: being rooted to the spot! You stood strong like a tree in the storm, and you stood strong with John just now. You didn't let him draw you into a fight. The game knew when you figured it out—otherwise, we'd still be back there, waving our branches around."

"This is the first time in my life I didn't get sucked into a fight," Alex said. "I'm always getting suspended for fighting."

"Standing like a tree needs to be practiced," Stephen said. "You never know when someone like John might set you off."

"How do you practice?" Alex asked.

"I'll explain it later. But what about the game—wasn't it amazing?"

"What was really cool," Alex said, "was how we could read each other's minds!"

Alex had never experienced such realistic virtual reality. The Wii3D-VR didn't come close. He liked games that needed a lot of practice, like flying drones or playing Scrabble, but this was different. You had to learn to control yourself from the inside out.

Stephen realized that he was also learning something: how to talk to people. He'd always had a rough time at school. The other kids made fun of his electronic voice or mocked his chair. And if they weren't making fun of him, they pitied him or ignored him like he was invisible, which was even worse. Sometimes girls would go out of their way to be nice to him, but it was usually to make themselves feel good, or to look good in front of others. They didn't really want to be friends with him.

With Alex, though, it was different. There was something about him that put Stephen at ease. When they were together, Stephen wasn't worried about his voice. It was as if they had known each other their entire lives.

At that moment, Stephen decided that he wouldn't just tell Alex how to practice Standing Like a Tree—he would invite him to his Tai Ji class.

As Alex walked home, the VR trip to China began to seem like a dream. He was unlocking the door when his watch-mii chimed. *I have to go to dinner with clients tonight*, his father messaged. *I picked up a pizza for you. Don't forget to brush your teeth before bed.*

Alex went into the house. The pizza box was on the kitchen counter, still steaming hot. After four pieces of feta and pineapple pizza and an hour of practicing Animal Royale on solo mode, Alex forgot all about his crazy day. Too tired to brush his teeth, he went straight to his room and lay down on his bed. Seconds after his head hit the pillow, he was asleep.

# CHAPTER 9

## *The Golem*

Next week, the two boys headed down Jefferson Avenue. It seemed like every person in New York had decided to go for a walk. The sidewalks were packed with bustling hordes, but Stephen nimbly navigated his chair through the crowd. Alex walked next to him, looking at all the people. They were pedaling bikes, walking dogs, and riding Segways. He even saw a policeman on a horse. A few service robots were out getting groceries for their owners while delivery drones whizzed overhead, carrying packages to their destinations.

Stephen was as nervous as a cat. He had never invited anyone to his Tai Ji class, and he wanted Alex to like it as much as he did.

Alex was looking in the shop windows. A Chinese grocery displayed ducks hanging over arrays of fresh vegetables and herbs. An electronics store showed flat-screen TVs playing scenes from the newest gamer-cinema experience—*Star Wars* Episode 26 for PlayStation VR 8. A butcher shop advertised lab-grown sausage links and steaks with the slogan: *Now with grass-fed taste!*

Stephen remembered the first time his mom took him to the

Tai Ji studio four years earlier. He had talked her ear off after wandering into that first class, and the next day she offered to take him for lessons of his own. At first, he was nervous, wondering how he would do Tai Ji in a wheelchair, but Dr. Bingze figured out how to adapt the ancient martial art for Stephen. Over time, he taught Stephen how to use his wheelchair to his advantage. "Always remember," his teacher said, "that sometimes what others see as your greatest weakness can become your greatest strength." Stephen was hooked. The studio became his home away from home, and Dr. Bingze was almost like a father to him. Stephen hung on to his every word and followed his every move. Doing this, he learned more and more about the mysterious strength of his body, wheels and all.

Stephen looked up at Alex and took a deep breath. "Here we are. Let's do it."

The boys entered the building and went to the elevator. Alex had never seen an elevator that looked like a big cage suspended on a wire. *This thing must be a hundred years old*, he thought. *Dad would love it.*

The elevator creaked and rattled as it lowered them to the basement. They stepped off and walked down the hall to the metal door at the end. Alex peered through the smudged window in the door. He saw people in a big room with mirrors on all the walls but one. On that wall hung a Chinese rug with ornate patterns of blue, red, and gold. The people were moving together in a slow, dreamlike sequence.

*It's just like in the picture book in my room!* he thought. He hadn't put it together until now, but he realized that he had seen this kind of movement before. It must have been when he and his dad were in China.

They entered the gym just as the class ended. A short, athletic

Chinese man waved and came over to the boys. "Hi, Stephen. Who have you brought to class?"

"This is my friend, Alex. He just moved here from England. He'd like to try a lesson!"

"There's no such thing as trying." Dr. Bingze smiled. "There's only doing or not doing." He turned to Alex. "Will you try not to try, and just do?"

"Uh, I guess." Alex nodded, uncharacteristically shy and slightly confused. "Er, I mean, yes, sir." He put his hands together and bowed slightly, like a Hollywood ninja before an epic fight. He immediately felt stupid. But to his relief, Dr. Bingze bowed back. Then he went to the front of the gym and announced the beginning of the next class.

About a dozen kids of different ages lined up in front of the mirrors. They were all wearing goggles, and they all greeted Stephen with friendly smiles.

"This is my friend, Alex. Anyone have an extra pair of goggles?"

One of the boys rummaged around in his sports bag and handed Alex a pair. Alex put them on, and the internal display instantly lit up. As he looked at the other kids, their names and class numbers appeared over their heads. Most of them were beginners like Alex—only year one or two—but a few had threes and fours next to their names. Alex didn't know it, but above his head, the word *xīnshēng* appeared—Chinese for "new student."

Dr. Bingze was standing at the front of the room with his legs apart. He placed his hands in front of his body, palms facing the floor—the starting position for Tai Ji practice. The students mirrored his position. Stephen and Alex found places somewhere in the middle. A red outline of the boy in front of Alex appeared in his goggles.

"Just follow the kid in front of you," Stephen whispered.

Alex nodded.

"Goooood," Dr. Bingze said. "Breathe in, breathe relax. Settle in."

The teacher's voice made Alex feel calm. He felt his breath slow down and get deeper. He relaxed.

When Dr. Bingze began the first move—Parting the Wild Horse's Mane—the red outline of the boy in Alex's display emulated Dr. Bingze's movements. Alex mimicked the moves, and as he did, he noticed that parts of the boy in his display would turn green when he got the moves right. *It's a guide!* he realized, trying his best to "not try."

Dr. Bingze had his own display, which allowed him to help students individually when they weren't quite getting the moves. As he led the class, he occasionally walked over to one of the students and corrected his or her form until their red highlighted areas turned green. He'd already helped Alex twice.

As the class went through other, colorfully named moves— Grasping the Bird's Tail, the Snake Creeping through the Grass, the Needle at the Bottom of the Sea—Alex began to enjoy himself. He knew he was a klutz. Tai Ji was harder than it looked, but it was fun to imagine himself grasping the bird's tail, creeping through the grass, and lying at the bottom of the sea.

Class ended. Dr. Bingze bowed to the students, and they bowed to him. Stephen looked at Alex. "So? How was it?"

"Cool! I want to come back."

"This is just the beginning. The adult class is next. They'll be sparring with the golems. Want to stay and watch?"

"Sure," Alex said. "What's a golem?"

"Follow me."

At the back of the gym, there was a large, arched doorway covered by a curtain. Stephen pulled it aside to reveal another room even bigger than the one they had just practiced in. Along the far wall were six bowling-pin-shaped alcoves.

Stephen led Alex to the middle one. Alex jumped, startled. Inside was what looked like an enormous gray statue of a man.

"That," Stephen said, "is a golem. It's a sparring robot. The adults use them to strengthen their form."

The golem had opaque, rubbery gray skin. Its body was featureless, save for some slight rounding where the muscles should be. Its hands were like mittens, fingerless but with a thumb, and its face was blank, like a mannequin's. Alex thought of a picture he'd seen of the Moai heads on Easter Island. He shivered. Even though golem gave him the creeps, he was intrigued.

"They're programmed to seek out human targets," Stephen explained. Alex's eyes widened. "Sometimes the adults sparring with them get whacked real good!"

"This is like having stormtroopers in the gym." Alex shuddered. "They must weigh three hundred pounds."

The adults in the next class began filing in. "Come on," Stephen said. "Let's go find a place to watch from." He wheeled his chair to the other side of the room, but Alex stayed close to the wall. He had had a big problem with the "heel kick" in class, and he wondered if it would help to practice it close to a wall. "Left knee up . . . and kick," he murmured.

He lost his balance. He desperately jumped on the right foot, his arms flailing. His hand found a handle sticking out from a big yellow panel, which broke his fall. The handle dropped down with a clang and Alex hit the floor. He scrambled back up just as the golem in front of him started to whir. The hair on the back of Alex's neck stood up. The giant shuddered, and two bright yellow lights lit up in the place where people have eyes.

Alex panicked. He tried to stop the golem by pulling on

another handle. There was another clang, and the yellow eyes of another golem flashed on.

In the meantime, Stephen realized that his friend wasn't following him. Just as he turned his chair around to see what Alex was doing, two golems stepped out of their alcoves, scanned the room, locked onto Stephen, and sped toward him.

To Alex, the next few seconds lasted forever.

Instead of trying to escape the golem, Stephen moved *toward* the closest one. A scream choked in Alex's throat, "NOOOOOOO!!!" Without thinking, he ran to help his friend.

Dr. Bingze ran into the room. He sprinted toward the golem, but it was too late. The things attacked the boy. Stephen yielded to the blow, and Alex thought his friend was done for. But at the last second, Stephen somehow changed the direction of the impact. The first robot's arms flailed in the air. It missed Stephen, who was still leaning out of his chair and swirling in a graceful arc behind the two golems. As soon as he got behind the second one, the robots smashed into each other with a dull thud. Alex and Dr. Bingze also collided with each other and crumpled into a heap. When Alex opened his eyes, he realized that his head was in his teacher's armpit. Horrified, he scrambled to his feet. Dr. Bingze rolled onto his back and laughed.

Stephen wheeled around with a crooked, impish smile. He was proud of himself for dodging the golems, which had now gone into standby mode.

Alex scrambled to his feet, wondering how Stephen had managed to avoid not one but both of the hulking monsters Alex had mistakenly unleashed. He steadied himself by grabbing the armrest of Stephen's chair. As the boys' hands brushed, Stephen's computer began beeping. The screen flashed: YIELDING AND REDIRECTING.

"Uh-oh! Oh, here we go again." Stephen sighed.

Alex looked around the room. Once again, time stopped. Dr. Bingze lay on the floor in front of them, frozen mid-laugh. Alex reached down instinctively as Stephen grabbed his hand. The gym shattered into millions of tiny glittering cubes, and the boys were sucked through the screen in a sparkling river of light. Then everything went black.

# CHAPTER 10

## *Yielding and Redirecting*

Wherever they were, it was hot and humid. Slowly, the darkness gave way to light, and the boys' eyes began to adjust to their new surroundings.

Stephen looked around and gasped. "A bamboo jungle! We must be back in China—as if we haven't had enough excitement for one day!" A breeze blew through the forest, rustling the leaves that covered the ground. The creaking and clicking of the bamboo echoed through the wood.

"Did you know that bamboo is actually a grass?" Stephen said.

But Alex's mind was still in the Tai Ji class. "How did you avoid getting creamed by the golems?" As he spoke, he realized that something was very different about his voice. "And why do I sound like a Wookiee?" He looked at Stephen and laughed in astonishment. "We're pandas!"

"We'll have to grin and BEAR it, I guess." Stephen shrugged.

Alex rolled his big, brown panda eyes. "Very punny," he said. And then he tackled Stephen. Their panda bodies were so fuzzy, it was like rolling around inside a pillow. The boy-bears chased each other through the bamboo forest, romping and dodging this way and that.

They came to a grassy clearing speckled with wildflowers at the foot of a great, rocky mountain. They collapsed onto their backs and looked up at the sky, out of breath. It was a clear sunny day. The sky was filled with puffy clouds that towered up, up, up, as far as the eye could see.

Alex pointed a furry paw at the sky. "That cloud looks like a pterodactyl!"

"And that one looks like a dog wearing a hat!" Stephen said. They laughed.

"What do you think the puzzle will be this time?" Alex asked.

As if a switch had been flipped, the earth began to tremble violently. They both jolted upright and looked at each other, wide-eyed with horror. Dozens of boulders were tumbling down the mountain straight toward them! This was no Tai Ji picture book.

"Run for the forest!" Stephen yelled. He rolled onto his side and dashed in the direction of the bamboo, bounding across the clearing on all fours and trampling wildflowers as he went. *So, this is what it feels like to run*, he thought. *It's amazing! I'm running from a rockslide, but it's fun!*

Alex was quick on Stephen's heels, reading his thoughts. He, too, was surprised by how natural it felt to be galloping across a field on all fours after a lifetime of getting around on human feet.

At that moment, a boulder the size of a refrigerator screamed past them and hit a shallow hole in the ground, which sent it curving into the air. It landed with a sickening crash in front of the boys, crushing a smaller boulder in two. Stones of all sizes were streaking past them as they ran toward the forest. Alex looked over his shoulder. The end of the boulder storm was nowhere in sight.

*Into the bamboo!* Stephen thought. Then he screamed aloud, as if that would make them run faster. "Into the bamboo!"

But Alex resisted. *We don't have a chance! The avalanche will mow down the bamboo—and us with it!*

Stephen was confident, though. *To stop a big force, maybe we need to bend and yield first! Like with the golems!*

*Bamboo definitely bends,* Alex thought. *And besides, we don't have much of a choice!*

The rumble behind them grew to a roar. The boy-bears ran into the forest just as the first rocks slammed into the bamboo stalks at the edge of the clearing. They ran harder, deeper into the forest, where the bamboo was bigger and stronger. There was crashing behind them as the boulders snapped the bamboo stalks. Alex was so scared—he couldn't control his thoughts. "We're done for," he cried—and tripped on a root.

He flew forward and crumpled to the ground. He knew full well he was about to get crushed by the boulders, but when they hit the bamboo behind him, the stalks didn't snap. They bent under the force and then sprang back, launching the boulders in the opposite direction. The huge flying rocks collided with the oncoming ones, forming a wall of rubble that stopped the avalanche in its tracks.

Alex let out a sigh of relief—though as a panda bear, his sigh sounded more like a snort. *Yield and redirect,* he thought, *like bamboo that bent down and sprang back.*

When Alex tripped, Stephen had felt the same adrenaline rush as his friend, so he waited for his breath to slow down before he spoke. "You asked how I handled those golems in the gym. Well, now you know. I yielded like bamboo. Then I pushed like a bear."

"Makes total sense," Alex said. "Before every good push, you yield to the oncoming force. I've always smashed right into it. Even if I 'won' the fight, I got creamed as much as the other guy."

Stephen raised his paw and gave Alex a high five. "Like Dr. Bingze says, every good yield lets you send the force right back to your attacker."

A breeze ruffled the fur on Alex's panda face. He looked at Stephen and noticed that his friend's fur was blowing away. Alex felt his own fur blowing away, exposing the skin underneath. The bamboo forest swirled and melted into inky blackness.

The boys were back in the gym. The two golems were in standby mode, their yellow eyes blank. Still laughing, Dr. Bingze got up from the floor.

"That was a close call," Alex whispered to Stephen. They

grinned slyly at each other—their friendship cemented.

"Stephen," Dr. Bingze said.

"Yes, sir?"

"Bring Alex to class early next time. We need to go over the golem safety procedures."

"Yes, sir."

"Uh, I'm sorry, Dr. Bingze." Alex said. "I can be really clumsy sometimes."

The teacher smiled. "Tai Ji will help with that. See you next time."

Alex's watch-mii chimed. "Dad wants me home. See you tomorrow, panda bro."

"For sure, pandamigo." Stephen grinned.

As Alex left the gym, he heard Dr. Bingze talking to his next class about yielding, bending, and redirecting. "Learning how to yield and redirect the force in real life never gets boring. Why? Because it takes a lifetime!"

# CHAPTER 11

## *Eagle Wing Whip*

The morning started with a storm coming from the Hudson River. Alex got up groggily and shivered as his feet touched his bedroom floor. He rubbed his eyes and yawned, scratching his shoulder. He was wearing his favorite rocket-ship pajamas. He loved it when spring was cold enough to actually wear pajamas. He slid his feet into his fleece-lined slippers and stumbled downstairs for breakfast with his father.

Before Alex knew it, he had finished eating, gotten dressed, said goodbye to his dad, and walked to school. He was halfway through his first class, Language Arts, learning about semicolons. The example sentence was about a superhero. The teacher, Mrs. Rethland, was calling on students to point out where the semicolon should go. A graphic image projected on the whiteboard at the front of the room showed an athletic woman with a mask and cape running across the top of a building. As she ran, the words of the sentence lit up below her.

Mrs. Rethland read the sentence aloud and said, "Who can tell me where to put the semicolon?"

Several hands went up, but the teacher called on a brunette in the front row. "Yes, Felicity?"

*Mrs. Rethland always calls on her,* Alex thought. A few other kids groaned; apparently, they felt the same way.

With her perfect posture and perky pigtails, Felicity said, "The semicolon should go between 'rooftop' and . . ."

Alex stopped paying attention. He looked out the window at the city; the storm was still brooding. The school was only three stories tall, so the surrounding buildings towered over it. Alex imagined himself outside, jumping from rooftop to rooftop and rounding up villains.

His daydream was cut short by the bell. "Be sure to watch the comma video before the next class!" Mrs. Rethland said.

Alex swiped the English workbook off of his screen and tossed it in his backpack. As he headed down the hall to American History class, he tried to remember what they were studying. Something about dressing up like Native Americans and having a tea party. It sounded like a scene out of *Alice in Wonderland*.

Just then he saw Sophia putting a sweater in her locker. She saw him, too. "Hi, Alex!" She tossed her shining curls over her shoulder.

"Hey, Sophia." Alex leaned against the lockers with his elbow, trying to look cool, but he slipped and banged his face.

"I thought crows were supposed to be graceful," Sophia laughed.

"Ow! More intelligent than graceful, I guess." Alex tried for a winning smile as he rubbed his cheek. His pride was only slightly bruised. He was glad he'd made Sophia laugh, but he wished he'd done it by being funny instead of clumsy.

"How are your classes so far?" she asked.

"Okay. I just got out of Mrs. Rethland's."

"You'll need those crow-brains to pass Language Arts!" Sophia joked.

An angry voice boomed behind Alex. When he turned around, he was facing John.

"Who said you could talk to my girl, *pollo* boy?" John jabbed his index finger in Alex's chest.

Wondering if "*pollo* boy" meant "chicken boy" in Italian, Alex said, "Uh, I'm pretty sure Sophia did. But I have to admit, I don't have it in writing."

"Leave him alone, John!" Sophia said. "We were just talking about—"

John cut her off. "You don't *ever* talk to her! In fact, if I see you around her or any of my friends, you'll make me very, very angry." John jabbed Alex in the chest again. "And you don't want that, *capiche*?"

Silence fell in the bustling hall. The students froze, waiting to see what would happen next.

A familiar fury grew in Alex's belly, snaking up his chest. Who did this little king think he was? But as his fists curled into tight balls, he remembered his and Stephen's adventure in the Chinese mountains. *Stand like a tree, stand like a tree, stand like a tree*, he reminded himself. He relaxed his hands and put them in front of his chest, turning his palms toward John to signal that he didn't want trouble. "I'm not going to fight you."

"Just what I thought—a *pollo* boy." John grabbed Alex's arms, and as Alex tried to free himself, John shoved him against the locker. Once again, Alex found himself with his cheek jammed into a metal door. "John, let him go!" Sophia said.

"I'm not chicken," Alex said. "It's just not worth it to fight."

"Fine!" John flung Alex on the metal locker again. This time it hurt. "Just remember what I said, *pollo* boy."

Alex watched as John's friends gathered around him, laughing. "You sure did teach the new boy a lesson, John," Roger said.

In spite of being upset, Alex noticed something strange in Roger's tone of voice, which made him wonder if Roger was mocking John.

John didn't notice anything strange. He turned to Sophia. "C'mon, *bella*."

Sophia looked at Alex, concerned, as she took John's hand. She kept glancing over her shoulder at Alex until she disappeared around the corner with John and his friends.

Holding his throbbing cheek and feeling the eyes of the other kids on him, Alex grabbed his backpack and ran to the nearest lavatory. He dove into a stall, tears of anger running down his cheeks. Exploding, he punched the door. "*Uuurrrraagghhh!*"

Then he had a terrible thought, a thought that stung more than his bruised cheek. *What if Sophia thought I meant she's not worth fighting over?* He took two deep breaths and left the bathroom for his next class. The rest of the day went by in a blur.

After school, Alex and Stephen met up at the flagpole. "My house or yours?" Stephen asked.

"Yours," Alex said. He didn't feel like going home.

As the boys headed to Stephen's apartment, Alex relayed the morning's events. "I wanted to fight back *sooooo* bad!" he groaned. "The whole time John was in my face, I just tried to stay rooted. I kept telling myself to stand like a tree!"

Stephen laughed. "You should have started chanting out loud! Stand like a tree! Feel your roots! Do not try, only DO!"

Alex smiled. "John would have been so weirded out, he and his gang would probably leave me alone forever!" The boys shared a belly laugh before returning to the problem—what to do about John.

Finally, Stephen said, "You were right not to fight him, but Tai Ji doesn't teach us to take beatings. It's a martial art, after all. We're not supposed to start fights, but if someone attacks us, we can redirect our opponent's energy against him."

"But how could I have used John's power against him? He had

my hands in a vice grip!"

"Actually, I know just the thing—the Eagle Wing Whip," Stephen said.

"The Eagle Wing What?" Alex looked at Stephen with an arched eyebrow.

"You know Dr. Bingze basically invented wheelchair-style Tai Ji for me, right?"

"No, I didn't know." Alex's respect for his teacher deepened.

"Well, anyway, there's a move he taught me early on that I think would work in that situation. Dr. Bingze called it the Eagle Wing Whip."

Alex imagined an eagle with a martial arts headband doing flying kicks. He hunched up his back, spread his arms like wings, and did a jumping kick as an impression. Stephen laughed, glad to see his friend's spirits lifting.

"I'll teach it to you when we get to my house," Stephen said.

Stephen's house was empty, his mom still at work when the boys arrived. Stephen poured them each a glass of lemonade, and they munched on graham crackers straight from the box. Then Stephen rolled his chair into the living room, they pushed the sofa up to the window, which created a nice open area for Tai Ji practice. Alex stood in front of Stephen.

"Dr. Bingze says you have to make your mind so calm, you can feel the movements of your opponent before he makes them."

Alex was skeptical. "Sounds like a superpower."

"That's what I said," Stephen agreed. "But Dr. Bingze says it's just a matter of learning to feel."

Alex nodded, but his expression said, "I'll believe it when I see it."

"Here," Stephen offered. "Put your hand on my fist and move with me." Alex placed his hand on top of Stephen's fist. Stephen slowly moved his hand in a circular motion, back toward himself and out toward Alex. Every now and then, he changed the direction of the circle. Paying close attention, Alex began to sense when Stephen was about to change direction.

His eyes widened. "Ah, I see."

"Of course, it's harder if you're not touching," Stephen said. "But you get the idea. Now let me show you the Eagle Wing Whip. Take my arms the way John took yours. Then try to shove me."

Stephen stuck his arms out. Alex hesitated at first, but then he grabbed Stephen's forearms the way John had grabbed his. He was about to shove Stephen when Stephen—instead of pulling back to try to free himself—followed the force and moved forward. Then he bent his arms and whipped his hands in a circle back toward Alex. Alex lost his balance and flew backward, landing on the floor. It was the second time he found himself losing his balance in one day, but this time, he was happy about it.

"Wow, that's incredible!" Alex said. "How did you do that?"

Stephen was still holding his hands out in follow-through, but he broke his pose and grinned at Alex.

"Now me!" Alex said.

Stephen went through the move several times so Alex could see each step. "Remember: feel, yield, and redirect. The move is circular, like all Tai Ji moves." Stephen gripped Alex's forearms. "Now try it on me." Alex rotated his arms, bringing them forward and around in a circle, escaping Stephen's grip.

They practiced the move until Alex got the hang of it and Stephen was being rolled backward in his chair by Alex's follow-through.

"Good!" Stephen said. "Now again."

# CHAPTER 12

## *Going Fishing*

That spring, Stephen helped Alex with his Tai Ji moves, and Alex taught Stephen the great game of chess. They constantly hoped for another surprise adventure into the ASP, but uneventful reality made for uneventful virtual reality. Alex avoided John and Roger, so there had not been a need for Eagle Wing Whip. Sophia was as friendly and pretty as ever—from a distance. Alex got the feeling she was avoiding him.

The most interesting development for Stephen and Alex was their progress with the crows. Once the frigid weather began to thaw for spring, they started teaching Jack, Jackie, and Jackleen how to draw with a ballpoint pen. Stephen thought they were smart enough to make bird art—or "bart," as he coined it. So far, they had wasted a lot of pens for only a few scribbles, but both boys were optimistic. One Saturday as they were sitting in the park, Stephen said, "When a crow caws, it's only communicating with one other crow. See? Jackleen is talking to Jackie, not to Jack."

"Stephen, you're imagining things."

"No, I'm not. Look at this visitor talking to Jackleen. His head is moving and he's cawing only to her. It's like in Tai Ji. You focus on one opponent at a time."

"Look, Stephen, the visitor must have been telling Jackleen he needed to poop. He just made a big one!"

They laughed, but then Stephen was serious again. "That would be the best way of communicating—to talk to someone else like I talk to myself."

"I love you, dude," Alex said, "but I don't really need to know every time you have to poop."

Sophia appeared from nowhere. "Hey, guys, what's up?"

"Oh, we're just watching the crows." Alex tried to sound casual, but his stomach lurched at the sound of her voice.

"Jackleen's the only one who's figured out how to get suet from the woodpecker feeder," Stephen observed.

"Maybe the others are lazy," Sophia suggested.

"Naw," Alex said. "Jackleen's the best with the key. She has a mind like an engineer."

"Keep at it, guys. Who knows—maybe one day you'll be able to charge admission! I've got to go, or I'll be late for swim practice. We are starting in the outdoor pool today. Bye."

The boys watched her until she disappeared.

New York got unseasonably hot, so one lazy Saturday in early May, Dr. Lasko decided to take the boys fishing. At first, Stephen's mother didn't want him to go, worried that Stephen's expensive computer would get wet. Dr. Lasko promised that he would take special care to keep both Stephen and his computer safe, and she finally relented.

"Here's the numbers where I can be reached," she said as Stephen got settled in the car. "And don't hesitate to call. In fact, why don't you call every hour to tell me how the trip is going? And Stephen, promise me you won't touch any fish. There's no telling what kinds of bacteria they might be carrying."

Dr. Lasko politely told her that phone service would be spotty at the lake, so they finally settled on one call to be made sometime that afternoon. For two boys accustomed to city life, a trip to a lake was a huge adventure. The car ride was an adventure in itself. Instead of an electric, self-driving cab, Dr. Lasko had insisted on driving the old wood-paneled, gas-powered PT Cruiser that he kept in a dusty storage garage near their house. Alex thought it smelled weird on the inside.

"Are you sure it's safe?" he asked.

Laughing, Dr. Lasko patted the dashboard. "This car is a classic. Built like a tank! My father used to take me fishing in it. When I turned sixteen, he gave it to me. I took your mom on our first date in this baby." A wistful look shadowed his face. Alex, who was riding in the front seat, turned away to look out the window. The sudden mention of Alex's mother surprised Stephen; Alex never talked about her. A sad silence fell over the car.

Alex changed the subject. "Dad, I've been meaning to ask you about a book I found in the attic, but something always comes up and interrupts me. It's a really strange book. It's in English, but also in Chinese—sometimes."

"Great!" Dr. Lasko said. "That'll help you learn Chinese. I've been lax about your lessons, but it's high time we . . ."

As Dr. Lasko was describing the verb structure of Chinese, Stephen rifled through the pocket on the back of Alex's seat. He found a map of Florida, a postcard of Mount Rushmore, a few coins covered in sticky brown goo, probably the remnants of a soft drink someone had spilled decades ago. Then he came across a dull gray block with a wheel-shaped button and a little screen on the front. Stephen could tell that the object had once been shiny chrome.

"What's this?" he asked, holding up the artifact.

Dr. Lasko stopped talking about Chinese long enough to look in the rearview mirror. His eyes lit up. "It's an MP3 player." He smiled. "Give it here. Alex, see if there's a cord in the glove compartment."

Alex found a dingy, tangled cord. Dr. Lasko plugged it into the bottom of the "pod," as he called it. Then he plugged the other end into the car's dash. He turned the knob on the old radio, and the tiny screen on the pod glowed brightly. The cool reggae beats of Bob Marley's *Legend* filled the car. Dr. Lasko grinned.

"I woke up 'dis mornin', to rise wit' 'de risin' sun . . ." Stephen and Alex looked at each other, unsure about the old music. Dr. Lasko was now singing along. "T'ree little birds! Is by my doorstep!" Stephen began to bob his head along to the beat. "Singin' sweet songs! A melody pure and full!" Alex caught the rhythm, too. "This. Is. My. Mess-age to you, hoo, hooo . . ."

They listened and sang for the rest of the trip. "Jammin'" was a particular hit. The boys thought the lyrics were *pajamas*, not we're *jammin'*. They thought it was so funny, Dr. Lasko decided not to correct them.

The Chinese book was once again forgotten.

Dr. Lasko rented a pontoon boat at the lake. Stephen rolled his wheelchair right on the boat from the dock. Dr. Lasko put Stephen's voice synthesizer in a special waterproof cover that hung from Stephen's neck and strapped around his chest. He made sure the cover was tight. Stephen could now drop his synthesizer to the bottom of the lake, and it would come out perfectly dry.

While Dr. Lasko loaded the fishing gear into the boat, the boys put on sunscreen and life jackets. Once they were all in, Dr. Lasko leaned over the motor and yanked the starter rope. It took a couple of tries, but the motor rumbled to life. Dr. Lasko gathered the boat's tie ropes, put one foot up on the dock, and shoved off. Then he took the wheel.

The boys settled on the seats behind him, playing chess on Alex's tablet as they put-putted across the lake. When they arrived at Dr. Lasko's favorite fishing hole, Dr. Lasko showed the boys how to bait their hooks with live crickets. The boys scrunched up their noses, laughing, grossed out.

"Okay, boys, listen up. When you cast your line, make sure your hook doesn't go *any*where near *any*body. Next, press this button with your thumb." He turned his wrist so the boys could see the push button on the back of the fishing reel. "Then pull your rod back like this and let her rip! Don't forget to release the button when you cast!"

Alex and Stephen took turns practicing. After a few near misses with wildly swinging hooks and renegade poles, they got the hang of it. They played chess while their fishing lines bobbed. Occasionally, one of them would get a nibble and scramble to reel the line back in, but the hook was usually empty. Once, Stephen reeled in what they all thought was a whopper, but it turned out to be a muddy stick dredged up from the bottom of the lake. It put up a good fight for a stick, though.

The fishing action was slow. The gentle sloshing of the water against the boat lulled them into a hypnotic state. Dr. Lasko practiced "boketto," the Japanese practice of staring off into space while thinking about nothing. The boys played chess.

"How did you get so good at this?" Stephen asked.

"The same way you got good at Tai Ji—practice. Dad taught me when I was six. He said it would 'discipline' my mind."

"Has it?"

"I guess." Alex shrugged. "Knight to C5! Check!"

Stephen grimaced. Once again, he was losing. Alex won all their games, but Stephen, with his concentration and steadiness, was learning quickly. Even so, he needed a break.

"Move like water, move like water," he murmured.

"Did you say something, Stephen?" Dr. Lasko asked.

"Dr. Peter?" Stephen called him this at Dr. Lasko's request. "Can we go swimming now?"

Dr. Lasko looked surprised. "Do you know how?"

"Yes! I love to swim. My spine transplant worked great for the upper body. I just need help getting back in the boat."

Dr. Lasko looked at Stephen, worried. "I don't know, Stephen. Your mother was very specific about you staying on the boat."

"*Pleeeease*?" Stephen smiled, silly and hopeful at the same time. "I'll leave my computer on the boat, so we'll talk with our hands."

*He does have a life vest,* Dr. Lasko reasoned to himself. *What could happen?*

"*Pleeeease*, Dad!?" Alex chimed in. "What's the fun of going to the lake if you can't get in it?"

Dr. Lasko sighed. "Okay," he said, "let's just make sure your life preserver is on good and snug. And put on your froggles."

"Yay!" both boys exclaimed. Alex hopped to his feet and tugged on his vest so his dad could see. Then he snapped his green frog goggles on and leapt off the stern of the boat, yelling, "Geronimo!" as he went in with a splash.

Dr. Lasko checked Stephen's life preserver. Stephen snapped on his froggles and wheeled his chair to the side of the boat.

"Cannon ball or slow dip?" Dr. Lasko grinned.

"Cannon ballllll!" Stephen yelled. He lifted himself out of his chair with his arms and landed in the water with a huge *kersploosh*. Then he disappeared. Several seconds went by. Dr. Lasko scanned the water with mild panic. All he saw were the ripples flowing out from where Stephen had gone in.

Suddenly, a squirt of water hit Dr. Lasko in the back of the head, and he turned around to see Stephen's goggled, grinning face laughing at him.

"I'm fine!" He gave Dr. Lasko a thumbs-up.

"Oh, you're going to get it for that, kid." Dr. Lasko yanked his T-shirt off and jumped in beside Stephen, spraying him and Alex with water.

To Dr. Lasko's surprise, Stephen was a great swimmer. He could not kick with his feet, but he made up for it in upper body strength. His shoulders were strong from pushing himself everywhere in his wheelchair.

After splashing and swimming, they lazed around in the water. Dr. Lasko grabbed a water noodle from the boat and wrapped it behind his back to buoy himself up. The boys bobbed around like apples in their life preservers. When they got hungry, Dr. Lasko hoisted Stephen back on the boat. Alex followed. They sat around eating barbecue potato chips and Tofurkey sandwiches with tomatoes, cheese, and pickles, and grapes for dessert.

To help "calm the fish down" after the boisterous swimmers invaded their world, Stephen dialed down the volume of his synthesizer, achieving what was, for him, a whisper. This made Alex and his father speak quietly, too.

Stephen lifted himself up with his arms close to the edge of the boat and bent over to look at his reflection in the emerald green of the lake. He dipped his hand in the water and swished it around, watching the ripples break up the smooth surface. In the distance, above the thick green of the tree line, the black silhouettes of the city's skyscrapers stuck up like fingers on a giant's hand.

Stephen looked at Alex, who was staring at a ladybug on his wrist. It opened its polka-dotted shell and flew off. Shaking his straight black hair out of his eyes, Alex turned his head to watch the ladybug fly away. A warm feeling of friendship and belonging overtook Stephen. He felt comfortable with Alex. It was a great feeling, to finally know friendship. It had just been him and his mom until now. He thought about his mom. He was lucky to have her, too.

Without thinking, he said, "Alex, was—is—your mom Chinese?"

Silence fell with a thud. Alex's face froze. Stephen felt sheepish and sick and wished he could take the question back.

"She . . ." Alex looked at his dad.

Dr. Lasko didn't say anything. He just stared at the floor of the boat.

"Yes, my mom was Chinese." Alex sighed. "She left a long time ago, when I was little. It's been hard for me and my dad."

"I'm so sorry, Alex." Stephen reached out to touch Alex on the shoulder. "I didn't mean to—"

Dr. Lasko put his hand on Stephen's own shoulder. "It's okay. You're Alex's friend. It's natural to wonder about his mother."

"And my father," Stephen shrugged.

Again, silence fell. Stephen mentally struck himself on the forehead. They had been having fun, fishing and swimming and lazing around, and then he had to go and bring up Alex's missing mother and his own missing father. Maybe he wasn't so good at this friendship thing, after all.

Alex also felt bad. He'd never given much thought to Stephen's lack of a father; he'd only thought of himself and how much he missed his mom. He decided to change the subject. "Stephen, why don't you show my dad some Tai Ji moves?"

"That would be great," Dr. Lasko said. "In China, I used to watch people practicing in the park."

"Okay," Stephen said. "Let's start with something called Standing Like a Tree."

Alex grinned, and Stephen felt better. Neither boy had told the other, but when they did this move, their thoughts traveled back to their first adventure in China.

Dr. Lasko seemed to catch on fast, Stephen noticed. He'd already closed his eyes to feel the move. After a few minutes, the boat became completely still. Stephen and Alex closed their eyes, too. When they all looked at the emerald water again, they felt peaceful. Alex's sadness about his missing mother, Stephen's about his missing father, and Dr. Lasko's about his missing wife— all their sadness was calmed by the simple sensation of feeling their roots grow deeper and their limbs reach toward the sky.

# CHAPTER 13

## *A Night in Town*

"Ding, ding!"

A customer walked into Yang's Chinese Grocery, and Stephen greeted her with a smile as he continued placing bags of noodles onto one of the many wire racks in the store. Yang's was on the other side of the block from Stephen's apartment. Mr. Yang and his mother had been friends ever since she and Stephen moved. And for the last two years, Stephen had worked for Mr. Yang a few hours a week. He did not do anything strenuous, and he liked helping the old man out. In return, the grocer gave him a little money here and there or paid him in groceries.

"Stephen? Could you stock the canned clams before you leave? They've been selling like hotcakes." Mr. Yang peered at the front window of his store. Then he pulled out a polishing rag and wiped something invisible off the pristine glass. He took immense pride in his business.

"Okay, Mister Yang. It's hard to believe that canned clams sell like hotcakes, but you're the boss. Um, I have Tai Ji practice today, so I have to leave a little early."

"In that case, skip the clams after you're done with the noodles. The last time Dr. Bingze was here, he told me what a good student you are. See you next week. Say hi to your mother for me."

"Will do, Mr. Yang!" Stephen beamed at the compliment. After stacking the last bag of noodles, he rolled himself around the block and met up with Alex. They made their way to the Tai Ji studio together.

Stephen and Alex stayed after class that evening. Dr. Bingze had agreed to give them some much-needed one-on-one instruction. Alex in particular was having trouble with some of the moves, even with the fancy headsets they wore. He hoped the extra coaching from Dr. Bingze would set him on the path to Tai Ji success.

"Alex, show me Rolling Down Like a Waterfall."

Alex furrowed his eyebrows. Rolling Down Like Waterfall was a graceful move that could throw an attacker off balance with only a little force. It looked simple, but it wasn't. Alex concentrated with all his might, which was a feat in and of itself. Teachers often accused him of being "hyperactive" or "lacking in focus." He couldn't disagree with them. He often felt like he would go crazy after hours of sitting in class—especially classes that bored him, like history. He would wake out of a daydream at the bell, realizing he hadn't heard a single word the teacher said. But Tai Ji, somehow, seemed to be helping.

His arms flowed, and he kept his abdomen strong as he performed the best Waterfall of his life. Even so, Dr. Bingze corrected him ever so slightly. Alex began again. He stood with his legs apart and put his hands out as if "repelling the monkey."

Then he moved his arms back and turned to his side with his arms out, as if holding a big ball to his chest.

"Stop," said Dr. Bingze. "Hold your position and look in the mirror."

Alex looked. A few months ago, he would never have guessed in a million years that he would know what he knew now. *Not bad*, he thought.

But again, Dr. Bingze corrected him ever so slightly, squaring his hips and adjusting his arms. Then he stepped away and said, "In real life, you will have to sense your attacker's intention! Only then can you defend. Your mind must be calm like a placid lake. Only then can you see the tiny ripples that your enemy makes."

Alex focused, hoping that one day he would be able to do the things Dr. Bingze described. Sensing another person's movements before they happened would be like magic! Alex practiced until Dr. Bingze was satisfied that he had a basic feel for the move.

"Good, very good. Before you go home, let's finish with Hands Like Clouds." Dr. Bingze went through the move slowly and the boys did their best to follow along.

"Good progress." Their teacher bowed, and the boys bowed back. With a friendly grin, Dr. Bingze said, "Time to go home. It's getting late. Glide like a crane over the mountains and you will have no adversity."

When Alex and Stephen got to the street, it was later and darker than usual. Alex thought the dimly lit street looked a little creepy. There were only two other people on it. But Stephen's apartment wasn't far, and his mom would be home by now, making dinner. Alex and Stephen had eaten at each other's houses so often that their parents didn't bat an eye when they both sat down at the table.

They were almost at the apartment when two figures up ahead

darted across the street and ran toward them. Alex went on high alert. The figures turned out to be two hooded teenagers who stopped in front of the boys. Neither Stephen nor Alex recognized them from school.

"Hey, what are you babies doing out past your bedtime?" This guy wore a thin sliver of a grin on his long face. Without speaking, he turned his head slightly to the side like a puppy, minus the cuteness.

"Actually, we're just getting out of Kung Fu class," Stephen said, trying to scare them off. He was pretty sure these goons had never heard of Tai Ji.

The idea of Stephen doing Kung Fu made the bullies double over in laughter. Stephen glanced up at Alex, whose fists were clenched.

The other teenager looked like a football player, but he had a baby face and an oily voice. "That's a nice computer." He pointed to Stephen's voice synthesizer. "What would you say something like that's worth, Nitro?"

"I dunno, Weezle. But I like it a lot. I think I want it."

Alex slowly reached over to grip one of Stephen's wheelchair handles.

"This thing?" Stephen tried to sound casual. "It's a gen-6 dinosaur. Freezes all the time, always bugging out. Terrible 3D graphics rendering. It was nice to meet you guys, though. Going home now."

"Sorry, but we can't let you do that," Weezle said. He lunged for Alex and tried to grab his arms, but Alex redirected the attack before he could even think about it. Weezle lost his balance and fell back, his head smacking onto the sidewalk. Nitro reacted quickly. He sidestepped his fallen comrade and went straight for the prize, Stephen's computer.

Stephen turned his chair at an angle and wheeled toward Nitro, freeing his arms from Nitro's clutch. He used Rolling Down Like a Waterfall, the move he and Alex had just practiced with Dr. Bingze, to redirect Nitro's forward movement. The wheelchair pivoted on one wheel in a graceful arc, speeding up Nitro's mass. Nitro lunged forward, head-first, and his face smashed into the cement.

Panting, Alex and Stephen grinned at each other, sharing a moment of triumph. But Weezle groaned and reached back to lift his head up. Nitro was pushing himself up with his arms. Alex and Stephen looked at each other, alarmed.

As Stephen retraced his mental map of the neighborhood, he remembered some stairs that went down to a basement. They were only about fifteen feet ahead on the left. He took off, pushing his chair as fast as it would go.

Alex didn't know what was going on, but he ran after the speeding wheelchair, trusting his friend's plan. When they reached the concrete stairwell, he looked at Stephen in horror. "You can't!"

Stephen was thinking the same thing. He had never taken his chair down more than a couple of stairs at a time. Now he was facing a narrow flight of about twelve. Before he could lose his nerve, he whipped himself around so his back was to the stairwell. He grabbed the handrails on both sides to steady himself, his eyes steely with resolve.

Alex glanced down the street. Their attackers were now on their feet and heading toward them. Alex didn't know what scared him more: Stephen's crazy plan or the approaching bullies.

Stephen took a deep breath. All he could hear were the rhythmic beats of his heart. He lunged backward, hurling his chair down the stairs. The wheels bounced as he descended, but he kept his balance by tightening his abdomen and holding onto the handrails. Just before he got to the bottom, his left hand hit a rusty spot and he cried out, more in surprise than pain. He had cut his hand, but he and his wheelchair were safely at the bottom of the stairs.

Alex bounded down after Stephen, ending up in a narrow, concrete alley. There were three doors on each side, all of them closed. Stephen sped to the end of the corridor, which widened into a truck loading zone. "Over here!" he cried. Alex ran.

The loading zone had three docks, each with a steel door that rolled up and down. Two of the doors were shut down tight, but the third was open halfway. The boys disappeared under the half-open door as the teenagers clattered down the stairs. "You kids are mine!" Weezle yelled. "I hope you've said your prayers!"

Shouting curses and threats, Nitro and Weezle banged on the locked doors.

The boys moved to the back of the bay, where they were engulfed in a shadow.

"Ooh! Hide-and-seek, is it?" Nitro taunted. "I *love* games."

Stephen and Alex disappeared behind a pile of boxes.

"We're in the back of Mr. Yang's grocery store," Stephen whispered. "I've known him ever since me and my mom moved here. He always leaves the back door cracked to air out the fish room at night."

Alex had not really heard him. He was too afraid to move, to talk, to breathe. The darkness was keeping them hidden—for now—but it still terrified him. Stephen winced and rubbed the palm of his hand. Now that the adrenaline had worn off, the cut throbbed with pain.

"Look, Weezle—a hidey-hole," Nitro said.

The teenagers stomped up the ramp. "Come out to play, little buddies! We'll have fun!" Nitro said.

*Crash! Clang!* Weezle and Nitro were turning over boxes to

flush out the boys. Weezle had found some sort of stick and was using it to poke in between the boxes. "Yeah! Let's play!" *SWACK!* Weezle kicked a bucket across the room.

Alex was trying not to think about all the things that could be lurking in the dark behind him. He shivered: Zombies! Or rats the size of cats. Or zombie rats!

Suddenly, Weezle's stick jabbed the stack of boxes Alex and Stephen were hiding behind. The screen on Stephen's computer flashed with a bright green light that spelled out: HANDS LIKE CLOUDS.

Nitro and Weezle's threats faded as Alex and Stephen fell into inky darkness, darker than any they had been in before.

# CHAPTER 14

## *Hands Like Clouds*

The boys were lying on a dirt floor. The air felt cool and moist. Alex's face was buried in the pelt of some animal. When he turned his head to breathe, he raised a hand to his face, but he couldn't even see a finger. It was dark, as dark as the night his mother left. Panic rose from his stomach to his throat in a howling spiral that threatened to choke the life out of him.

"We're in the game again," Stephen said.

"Feels different." Alex gasped. "Not a game."

"Are you okay?" Stephen reached out to reassure his friend, but he touched a wall of rock. "Where are you?"

"Here," Alex gargled.

Stephen tried again. This time, he found Alex's arm, but instead of touching his friend's sweatshirt, he felt fur. "Whoa. Definitely in the game." He let go of Alex's arm and touched his own; it was also furry. He patted himself all over. Whatever he was wearing, it was furry and held together with leather thongs. Animal skins? He thought about the history shows he had seen on TV.

"Alex, we're in a cave. We're wearing animal pelts."

Alex was scared and trembling. "We've gotta get out of here!" he whispered. "This place is probably crawling with snakes and spiders and bats. There could even be bears!"

"Shhh! Did you hear that?"

An unearthly moan echoed from deep within the cave. The boys panicked and scrambled to their feet.

"Feet!" Stephen crowed, astonished. "I can't believe it! I'm standing on my own feet!"

"Wow!" Alex was so happy for his friend, for a moment he forgot that he was afraid of the dark. "That's amazing!"

Stephen sighed. "For once, I wish the game would let me walk and see at the same time."

The unearthly moan started back up, this time rising to a howl. The boys grabbed each other's hands. The howl stopped, followed by words that bounced off the rocky walls. "Cave spirits-irits! I beg you-ou! My leg-eg! Help-elp!"

Alex dropped Stephen's hand and thrashed blindly about, looking for a ray of light to lead him out.

"Alex, WAIT! It sounds like an old man. He needs our help. We have to find him."

"Oh, sure!" Alex said. "When you're magically transported into a cave, you should go looking for the first moan you hear."

Stephen snickered, but he knew they would have to be extra careful. This might be exactly what the game demanded of them this time around.

The moaning was coming from somewhere behind and above the boys. "Pleeease, help me, most merciful spirits! Without you, I will perish."

"Okay." Alex sighed. "How will we find him? I can't even see my hand in front of my face!"

Stephen put his hand on Alex's shoulder to reassure him. "The same way I just found you. We'll follow the sound of his voice."

The friends were suspended at an odd moment. Not only had Stephen never patted Alex on the shoulder before—he'd never patted *anyone* on the shoulder. He'd never been able to reach that high. People patted *his* shoulder all the time, but this was the first time he was able to extend this simple gesture. Friends mostly grow closer over time. But occasionally something is shared that instantly deepens the relationship. This was one of those somethings. Alex's crazed fears subsided for a moment.

"Let's breathe," Stephen said, "like we do in class with Dr. Bingze." He slowly inhaled through his nose and exhaled through his mouth.

At the mention of Dr. Bingze, Alex calmed down even more. Dr. Bingze was a man he respected; he would never want his teacher to see him like this. As he breathed with Stephen, his quick, shallow breaths slowed down, and his frantic thoughts began to float away like leaves on a stream.

"Are you good?" Stephen asked.

"Better. Let's find this old man."

They headed toward the voice, carefully feeling their way along the cave wall. They heard the gurgling of a stream. The old man's groans seemed to be coming somewhere beyond it. The stream led the boys to the bottom of a waterfall.

"The stream must start above the waterfall," Alex said. The boys felt the wall for a path or foothold they could climb up.

"Maybe we can get up this way." Stephen grabbed Alex's furry shoulder and directed him to a crevice in the wall.

"Ugh! Awoh!" The old man moaned. "Oh, cave spirits, have pity!"

"You go first. I'll be right behind you," Alex said. "Hey, Mister! We aren't cave spirits, but we'll do our best to help you. Just keep talking so we can find you."

"Why do you tease an old man so? You know where I am! You ride the wind, so ride it to me!"

Stephen and Alex crawled into the crevice, then reached up, carefully feeling around for handholds and footholds. When they reached the top, they felt a breeze blowing from the direction of the old man's voice.

"Whew!" Stephen said. "I sure do hope we don't have to go back down." His voice echoed. "It sounds like we're in a cavern now."

"I think the old man's somewhere straight ahead," Alex said, "so we won't be able to use the wall as a guide. What if the sounds take us in the wrong direction? There's an echo in here." His breathing got fast again.

"We have to walk like Dr. Bingze told us to—like a cat."

"Good idea," Alex said breathlessly, trying to sound confident.

Stephen assumed a wide-legged stance. "Let's go. Listen to the cave and feel the ground with your feet. Shift your weight carefully and center your balance. And do 'Hands like Clouds' to feel the space in front of you."

They felt the way forward with their feet and hands. Stephen wasn't used to using his legs, but walking with the cave wind behind him was pure joy. He savored the feeling of standing on his own feet. No one could see, but his smile went from ear to ear.

The boys stepped lightly but deliberately. They waved their free hands slowly, like clouds floating in the sky, to keep their balance. They followed the old man's groans, but their own voices bouncing off the cave walls also helped them feel out the space.

"Echo!" shouted Alex, as he stepped forward with Tai Ji precision. "I think we're getting close to the wall. I can hear it." After a few more steps, his hands touched a hard, wet surface. He sighed with relief.

"Oh, cave spirits, bless you for taking pity on an old man! I'm here! But what's this? You two are more like boys than normal cave spirits."

*Impossible,* Alex thought. *No one can see in this blackness. How does he know we're here? And how can he tell we're boys, not spirits?* But instead of asking these questions, he asked, "What are *normal* cave spirits?"

The old man answered, "A blind old man need not see the world to know its workings. He must only listen!"

Suddenly, a spidery hand came out of nowhere and grabbed Stephen's arm. "Aagh!" he screamed.

"What are you boys doing in my cave, anyway? Are you from the river tribe?"

"We're . . . here . . . to help you," Stephen gasped. "We're from New York City."

"Noo-ork-sitty," the old man said thoughtfully. "I've never heard of that village. Well, no matter. Thank you for coming. You may call me Uncle Jian. I was hunting a saber-toothed rabbit when my foot got stuck in some rocks. Such is the life of an old man."

It was difficult to know what to do. The boys felt their way around and tried to figure out where the rocks were and where Uncle Jian's ankle was. He seemed to be pinned against the cave wall by a huge boulder.

"Why do you hunt alone, Uncle Jian?" Alex asked. "It's dangerous."

"Because this is where the wily saber-toothed cave rabbit lives, that's why! No one else will come after him. They're all sissies, afraid of the dark."

"And you?" Alex asked.

"I am blind, so it's all the same to me!"

Stephen found the old man's hairy ankle.

"Yowch! That hurts!"

"Sorry. Alex, if we pivot the rock, we'll be able to free him."

But the rock would not budge.

"We need the strength of three people," Alex said.

Uncle Jian spoke up. "Legs are stronger than arms."

"Uncle Jian, you're a genius. Alex, climb up with me to the top of the rock."

The boys climbed up behind Uncle Jian and slid between the giant rock and the wall of the cave. They squirmed to find their footholds.

"On the count of three," Stephen said, "push off the wall with your legs. One, two, three!" Together, they pushed off the cave wall with their backs to the boulder that held Uncle Jian's foot captive.

Alex gritted his teeth and pushed with all his might. Slowly but surely, the stone leaned away, grinding as it went.

"I can't take much more!" Alex cried.

"Just . . . a bit . . . further!" Stephen shouted through gritted teeth, relishing the strength in his legs.

The rock groaned under its own weight as it tipped onto its side, away from the wall. Alex and Stephen fell to the cave floor.

"I'm free! Hee hee!" squealed Uncle Jian. He grabbed the boys and gave them both a big bear hug. Both Alex and Stephen half smiled, half grimaced. The old man smelled awful.

"Now you boys can help an old man on his hunt!"

"How can you hunt on an injured foot?" Alex asked.

"Just give me a minute." Uncle Jian sniffed. "I've got a magic ointment for such occasions." A few moments later, the old man sighed. "Ahhh. Much better. Let's go! The wily saber-toothed rabbit is nearby. I can smell it!"

"But we don't know how to hunt," Alex said.

"Don't know how to hunt? What kind of elders do you have

in Noo-ork-sitty? How will you feed your families when you grow up? This must be remedied! Today, I will teach you to hunt!"

"In the dark?" Alex asked.

"The dark doesn't seem to bother you right now." The grin on Stephen's face could be heard in the tone of his voice.

Alex was startled. "Wow! You're right! I'm not scared." He paused. "Still, hunting for the first time would be easier if we could see."

"I'm such a silly old man! I forget that not all are blind. This will help." Uncle Jian cracked two things together and a spark of flame shot out, igniting the end of a torch that lay on the ground.

Light flooded the cave and illuminated Uncle Jian's wizened face. A thick brow hung over faded brown eyes that studied the boys with curiosity. From his chin flowed a scraggly white beard as long as Alex's arm. The old man smiled, showing yellow teeth as he lifted the torch and let loose a mighty bellow from his fur-clad chest.

The light from the torch bounced off every surface of the cavern. Alex and Stephen gasped as countless paintings of people and beasts jumped off the walls under the dancing flames. There were warriors hurling spears, women pounding grain, and children running alongside buffalo. There were paintings of giant birds twice as tall as a man. There were big cats with dagger claws, horned rhinoceroses, and gigantic woolly elephants. Pottery shards littered the floor.

"Follow me, boys," Uncle Jian said. "Today, you will learn the sacred art of hunting the saber-toothed cave rabbit."

Stephen and Alex could barely keep up with the old man, who scampered like a mountain goat over the rocks that occasionally blocked the path. Finally, Uncle Jian stopped. "Here, we set our trap."

He took off his leather rucksack and pulled out a cage woven from sticks. "Step one," he said, "set your trap." He rifled through the rucksack and brought out a turnip. "Step two, bait your prey. Cave rabbits love turnips. They collect them and keep them in their burrows for eating. Some say they are comforted by the smell."

The old man put the turnip in the cage and set the cage on the ground. "Follow me, boys." They quietly backed up to the cave wall and crouched down. After a few minutes, they heard a loud purr.

"That," Uncle Jian whispered, "is the purr of the saber-toothed cave rabbit."

Alex and Stephen tensed up, not knowing what to expect.

"Don't be alarmed. Cave rabbits are jittery creatures. They frighten easily and skitter away as fast as they can when they're surprised. But they can't resist the smell of turnips, which brings me to step three: make the rabbit think you're far from the trap. They're smart little creatures. They're as blind as I am, so they rely on their big ears."

Uncle Jian tossed a handful of pebbles across the floor, making a racket about a dozen yards away. The boys heard a scurrying sound. A streak of white zipped across the cave. Then there was a sharp snap.

"That, boys, is how it's done!"

Stephen and Alex walked over to the cage. The little rabbit sat curled up with the turnip in the corner, shivering. It had two short, blunt tusks that were cute rather than ferocious.

"What now?" Stephen asked. "Are you going to eat it?"

"Heavens, no!" Uncle Jian said. "I'm going to give it to my granddaughter as a pet. Saber-toothed cave rabbits are cuddly little things."

Alex and Stephen looked at each other, then at the rabbit. Uncle Jian stuck a finger through the cage to pet the little animal, and it began to purr again.

"Thank you for showing us how to hunt, Uncle Jian," Stephen said.

"Yes," Alex chimed in. "That was very . . . educational." He met Stephen's eyes. The boys were confused. What was the game trying to teach them? Hunting cave rabbits wouldn't be exactly useful in New York City. But handling one's fears by doing things you *need* to do? Yes!

The old man said, "It's good to keep learning. You never know what you might need to use someday."

The boys gasped, but Uncle Jian was still talking. "I also thank you, boys, for freeing me from that rock. The spirits were looking out for me when they sent you into the cave! Now I must go back to my village. Soon we will part ways."

There was no answer. "Hello?" he called.

All he heard was silence. The boys had gone. A shiver ran up the old man's back. "I was wrong," he said. "They *were* spirits."

# CHAPTER 15

## *The Stuck Door*

Alex felt the cold steel of Stephen's wheelchair in his hands. The boxes in front of him wobbled as Weezle and Nitro closed in. Alex was terrified again.

Thinking through the problem, he only saw one hope. He reached down and activated the screen on his watch-mii. If Alex called his father, he would come. They would have to take a beating, but maybe his dad would get here in time to catch the bullies in the act. He was about to press the call button on his watch when another idea hit him.

"Cave rabbits," he murmured. He tapped another button on his watch-mii, crouched down, and slid the watch across the floor. It came to a stop on the far wall.

"Why did you do that?" Stephen asked, but just then, Bob Marley's *Legend* began blaring from the other side of the room. "Could you be looooooved? Whoa now, then be looooved . . ."

The crashing stopped. Weezle and Nitro ran to the other side of the room, ransacking it for the source of the music.

"Go—fast!" Alex whispered frantically. "Wait for me behind the door."

Stephen sped around the pile of boxes, Alex only a few steps behind him. When they passed under the half-open door, Stephen said, "Now what?"

"We trap our cave rabbits." Alex grinned. His hand gripped the lever to the door. Nitro and Weezle turned around just as Alex pushed the lever down.

Nothing happened.

He pushed it again with all his might. Again, nothing happened. Alex looked up in horror. Nitro and Weezle were speeding toward them. "This is it." He gulped. "We're dead meat!"

But Stephen was shouting, "Your legs! Your legs are stronger!"

Alex bounded onto the armrest on Stephen's wheelchair and jumped on the lever to the door. Stephen's chair flew through the hallway just as the door began to fall. It rumbled down and shut with a thud, trapping the bullies inside.

The boys rolled down the ramp and stopped at the bottom. They stared at the closed door, mouths open and breathing heavily.

"We did it!" Stephen shouted.

Alex turned around to give him a high five. Grinning, they faced the garage door.

"Let us out! Now, or else!" Weezle yelled.

"My mom will kill me if I'm not home by ten," Nitro hollered.

The two hoodlums banged, shouted, kicked, and swore. The door rattled, but it wouldn't budge. Stephen called out, "Don't worry, guys. Someone will let you out—eventually."

Alex laughed. "Let's get out of here."

They walked down the alley to the front of Mr. Yang's grocery store. The windows were shattered, and glass littered the sidewalk. Food was strewn everywhere. Stephen was stunned, but an approaching siren flooded him with relief. A police cruiser pulled up with squealing tires. Two officers got out, one shining a flashlight, the other talking into his radio.

The one with the flashlight introduced himself. "I'm Captain Johnson. Are you boys okay?"

Alex and Stephen nodded.

"The guys who threatened you—which way did they go?"

Alex and Stephen looked at each other, wondering how the officer already knew about Nitro and Weezle. They pointed to the alley. "They're in the warehouse," Alex said. "You can hear them banging on the door."

Officer Johnson picked up his radio. "Unit 317 here. We're following up on a 240 at a Chinese grocery on Fifth and Main. We think there's a 459 in progress. Requesting backup. Over."

Within minutes, another cruiser pulled up, lights flashing. Two more officers got out. Alex and Stephen waited by the cars while the police headed down the alley. After a few minutes, the boys heard the warehouse door roll up. They heard Officer Johnson yelling "Freeze!" They heard pounding footsteps. They saw Nitro and Weezle sprinting, Officer Johnson and his partner lunging, and all four falling to the ground. They saw the other two officers cuffing the hoods and shoving them into a cruiser.

"You boys are lucky," Officer Johnson said. "We got several calls from people who saw them vandalizing the grocery store, and one from a lady who saw them trying to mug you." The officer tilted his head. "How did you manage to fight them off? They're pretty tough kids."

"I guess we're stronger than we look," Stephen grinned.

Officer Johnson grinned back. "Get in. I'll take you boys home."

"We're good. We live close by."

The policeman cocked an eyebrow. "Are you telling me you don't want to ride in a cruiser?"

The boys laughed. The officer helped Stephen into the car and stowed the wheelchair in the trunk. Alex climbed in back with his friend. "I think I'm over my fear of the dark," he said.

"We got so busy saving Uncle Jian, we forgot to be afraid."

"We moved that huge rock with our legs!" Alex shook his head as if he still couldn't believe it.

Stephen lit up. "Did you see Uncle Jian's face? He looked like Bigfoot!"

"So did you," Alex laughed. "I guess I did, too."

"Yep. I feel bad about Mr. Yang's store, though. He's going to be so upset when he sees what those two losers did to it."

Officer Johnson and his partner got in the car. "Mr. Yang is on his way here with his family to clean up. It's a big mess, but he probably has insurance."

"What about Nitro and Weezle?" Alex asked. "What will happen to them?"

The cruiser pulled away. "Those guys have quite a record. They'll probably end up in juvenile detention this time." The policeman turned around with a mischievous grin. "So, boys, ready to ride?"

"Yeah!" they said in unison.

Officer Johnson pressed a button and flipped a switch. With the siren wailing and the blue light swirling, the cruiser turned onto Atlantic Avenue. The traffic slowed down and pulled over. The cruiser picked up speed and went blazing down the street, the boys and the officers grinning from ear to ear.

# CHAPTER 16

## *The Trip to Arizona*

Word spread quickly around the school that Alex and Stephen had helped the police capture and arrest the hoods who had vandalized Mr. Yang's grocery, ransacked several video shops, and assaulted an old lady. Several versions of the story circulated. Because of the Tai Ji element, they included everything from Alex doing flying flip kicks to Stephen throwing "ninja stars" to pin the muggers to the wall. And because the boys were always together, people started calling them the Tai Ji Twins. They got admiring glances from the other kids, especially the girls, as Stephen was happy to remind Alex.

But most of all, Alex was happy that his father was proud of him for once. The incident brought him back from the cloud and the two were talking more often now.

"Dad, all this Tai Ji stuff started with the strange Chinese book I found in my room. It was hidden in a cubbyhole. The Chinese characters changed into English, and the pictures moved."

"Is it a tablet?" his dad asked.

"No, it's a book. A really old one full of magic! It's about a princess who—"

The telephone rang. Alex sighed as his father picked up.

"Hello? Lasko speaking. Oh, hello, Mr. Skeeter."

Alex groaned. His dad shushed him and put the phone on speaker.

"I've called to inform you that Alex's class will be taking a trip to the Grand Canyon soon. I'd like your personal assurance that Alex won't make any trouble."

Dr. Lasko was indignant. "Why? He hasn't done anything wrong! To the contrary, he helped apprehend two juvenile delinquents."

"I know, I know. I just want you to be aware that the hike is rugged. All the children will need to pay full attention so we don't have any accidents."

"Is that all, Mr. Skeeter?" Alex's father was upset.

"I just want to be on the safe side, Mr. Lasko."

"Good night, then." Alex's father hung up. Alex was excited about the trip. Nobody remembered the Chinese booklet.

Expectations mounted as the field trip to the Grand Canyon approached. The trip, Alex learned, was a school tradition that went back twenty years. Inexpensive coast-to-coast travel had been made possible two decades earlier by a supersonic train called the Hyperloop, which was less like a train and more like the pneumatic tubes at a bank teller's drive-through. The Hyperloop made the trip from New York to San Francisco in less than four hours.

Alex was excited about seeing the Grand Canyon. Of all the places he had visited with his father on their travels, they had never been out West, except to Los Angeles. He had heard they would take a balloon ride into the canyon. He hoped Sophia would be on his balloon. Then he frowned. John would be there, too, and he would make sure Sophia was on *his* balloon. Even so, Alex could barely contain his excitement. The Grand Canyon was one of the natural wonders of the world!

Things were a bit different at Stephen's house.

"No way, I won't sign this." Stephen's mother stared at the email. "Do you have any idea how dangerous those trails are?"

"But Mom! Alex is going. And remember, we fought off those teenagers! If I can defend myself on the streets of New York, I can wheel around some rocks."

"You're not going, Stephen," she snapped. She didn't like being reminded that Stephen and Alex had been jumped just a few blocks away from the apartment. But as she looked at her son's comically defiant face, her tone softened. "You're my strong boy, but I won't let you risk your life out in the wilderness. You have to be more careful than other kids."

To Stephen's horror, his mother clicked the email, sending the permission slip to the delete folder. He slumped in his chair, defeated.

"Missing one trip isn't the end of the world. You'll see Alex again when he gets back." His mother got up and left the room.

Stephen glowered. His whole life, everyone had been fretting over him, treating him like a glass figurine that could break at any moment. He was fed up with it. Now, once again, he was going to miss out on something huge. He was wallowing in self-pity when he noticed that his mother had not signed out of her email account. He peered around the corner to make sure she was gone.

The coast was clear. He rolled over to the keyboard. He hesitated. He had never done anything as brash as what he was about to do. But then he thought about what his mom had just said. *"You have to be more careful than other kids."* He clenched his jaw and took the permission slip out of the delete folder. Then he checked the "Yes, my child has permission to go" box, signed his mother's name, and sent the email to his teacher.

He wasn't going to miss this trip for anything. He would tell his mother he wanted to spend those three days with his cousin Jamie, who lived on the Lower East Side in Manhattan. She wouldn't object to that as Stephen often stayed with him over the weekend. She wouldn't suspect a thing.

The day of departure, everybody had to be at school early. Alex met up with Stephen at their secret spot in the park and they made their way to the main building, where they were sucked into the hubbub of teachers organizing hundreds of students for a long field trip. Some of the teachers were holding tablets and checking names off the roll. Others were counting bagged lunches and putting juice boxes into coolers. The rest were doing their best to corral students into orderly lines.

The bus ride to the Hyperloop station was short. Alex had seen it before, but he still marveled at it when he stepped off the bus. The station was shorter than the surrounding skyscrapers, but it was no less impressive. The glass roof was shaped like a turbulent ocean wave with shimmering peaks jutting up and out. There were no visible supports underneath, which made it look like the glass wave was floating in thin air.

Alex was taking it all in when Stephen rolled up. The boys swung into their favorite Tai Ji poses and stared each other down with ferocious warrior faces. As usual, Stephen was the first to laugh.

"Ha ha. You get me every time," he said. "How do you keep

your face so serious? Do you practice in front of the bathroom mirror every night?"

Alex shrugged and pretended to brush off his shoulder with an air of self-satisfaction. "A magician never reveals his secrets," he said, looking down his nose at his friend. Then he laughed and they fist bumped. "Let's do this," Alex said. They followed the rest of the class to the station.

It was packed. There was a group of well-dressed European tourists speaking a language that Stephen's computer identified as Polish. A young mother walked by with a set of toddler triplets; their small heads were encased in the blue glow of noise-canceling bubbles, a controversial new parenting device. A throng of beautiful Asian businesswomen scurried by, each followed by a tiny whirring drone.

And screens! So many screens. Alex wondered aloud how anyone could read the tiny letters that showed arrivals and departures. The Hyperloop terminals looked like giant tubes half buried in the ground. A Hyperloop pod in the terminal next to theirs slowly inched forward until it reached the takeoff point. Then with a "FOOMP!" it disappeared into the tube at hypersonic speed. Alex, Stephen, and some of the other kids in their group laughed at the sound. They heard the same muffled noise multiple times every few minutes as pods all over the station took off toward their destinations.

It was only a few minutes before their class's pod pulled into position and opened its doors. Everybody walked in and took their seats. Mr. Bandorro, one of the teachers, fastened Stephen's chair to the wall with the straps that were provided. Alex took a seat next to him.

The pod was sleek and mostly made of glass. A small robot shaped like a fire hydrant buzzed through the cabin instructing everyone to fasten their safety belts and remain seated during takeoff. When the doors hissed shut, Alex and Stephen looked at the glass ceiling to watch the tube close and lock into place. The pod slowly slid forward. A digital readout over the doors beeped three . . . two . . . one, and the pod shot forward so fast, the passengers were momentarily pushed back in their seats. Stephen imagined this must be what astronauts feel like when they are blasted into space.

The view out of the windows was dark, rhythmically interrupted by white streaks of service lights. It reminded Alex of the subway. But once they were above ground again, light blazed all around them. The tube, like their pod, was made of clear glass.

A few minutes later, the overhead speakers chimed, and a robotic female voice said, "The time is 9:40 A.M. Eastern Standard Time. Pod 4532 en route to Phoenix, Arizona, estimated time of arrival 10:40 A.M. Mountain Time. We have now reached a cruising speed of 704.2 miles per hour. Feel free to move about the cabin."

The din of seatbelts unclasping filled the cabin. Most of the students crowded around the windows to get a better view of the countryside as it zipped by. There was a gasp as the pod went underground again.

"Want to play chess?" Stephen asked. "There's a virtual board on the table tablet."

"Sure," Alex said. Stephen pushed a button on his armrest, and a tabletop unfurled from the wall like a scroll. He scanned the list of games and selected chess. The checkerboard pattern of a chessboard appeared on the surface, followed by thirty-two digital chess pieces. Two moves into the game, a shadow fell over the board. Stephen and Alex looked up to see John, flanked by two of his toadies.

"Can we help you?" Alex used his most sarcastic voice.

John bent down and squinted at the chess game. "How old are

you two—eighty? Just when I thought you two spazzes couldn't get any more pathetic, *BADABING*! I catch you playing a game for geezers. What's next? You going to race your walkers?"

John's toadies snickered at the insults. Then Ronald, the skinny one, pointed at Stephen. "This one can't even stand up, much less race."

Stephen looked at his hands in his lap, obviously hurt.

"You guys should learn how to play a man's game." John bent down again, muttered something Italian under his breath, and flicked one of Alex's digital knights off the board. The game animated the piece flying off the board and also played a ricochet sound effect.

Alex stood up, his fists clenched.

John got in his face. "What are you gonna do, *vigliacco*? Use some of those ninja skills we've heard so much about?"

"It's not worth it, man." Stephen put a hand on Alex's arm. "Just ignore them. Let's finish our game."

"Oh, *mio cuore*." John put his hand over his heart dramatically. "Saved by your *fratellino*."

By now Mr. Bandorro had spotted Alex and John in each other's faces and was walking over. "You boys have something you want to share with me?"

Roger put a hand on John. "Let's go, man. Let's go."

John gave Mr. Bandorro a charming smile. "*Maestro!* We were just talking about games!" He turned to walk away and shot a finger in the air. "*Avanti*! Let's go!" He and his toadies walked to the other end of the pod.

Mr. Bandorro bent his head forward and looked over his glasses at Alex. "I'm going to keep my eye on you two."

"But we were just playing chess!" Alex protested. "John started it!"

"With words," Mr. Bandorro said. "You were the one about to fight. If I see any more of that, you'll enjoy the rest of the trip at my side. Got it?"

Alex and Stephen nodded.

After the teacher went to his seat, Stephen said, "You can't let John rile you up so much! He'll push you into doing something you'll regret. Then you'll be stuck with Mr. Bandorro for the rest of the trip!"

Alex sighed and looked out the window. He had lost interest in the chess game.

"Hey, c'mon. Cheer up!" Stephen gestured to the chess board. "Best two out of three?"

Upon arrival in Arizona, the class was ushered off the Hyperloop and into the Phoenix station, which incorporated local geology into its design. The kids stared in wonder. The arrival platform was built inside a cave that had crystal stalactites hanging from the ceiling. The walkways from the platforms to the exits were glass tubes that burrowed through the rock formations of a small canyon system. The rock walls gave way to sunlight when the tunnel emerged from the earth again.

"Keep going, class!" Mr. Bandorro said. "We've got to make our flight!"

"Flight?" asked Alex, looking at Stephen in surprise.

"According to bullet point number four of Bandorro's email, we'll be riding a blimp into the canyon." Stephen shook his finger at Alex in mock admonishment. He often filled in the details that Alex missed or forgot.

As the class filed out through the gate one by one, Mr. Bandorro swept a laser scanner across each student's face to make sure everyone was present. A teenager in an orange "Grand Canyon Blimp Company" T-shirt was standing next to Mr. Bandorro, stamping each student's right hand.

Alex fidgeted with anticipation. He had just found out that he would be riding a blimp, only to get stuck in a bottleneck of adult supervision. "Hurry it up, Bandorro," he muttered. "No one's going to wander away from a blimp ride."

When Stephen and Alex got to the front of the line, Bandorro scanned the boys, hesitating just a moment before scanning Stephen. The teenager stamped their hands. "Have an awesome time in the grandest of all canyons, dudes!" he said, unexpectedly enthusiastic considering that he had already greeted over two hundred guests.

When they got through the gate, the students gaped at the giant blimps floating above.

"Head to bay four, class! BAY FOUR!" Mr. Bandorro bellowed. The kids rushed to the parked blimp, jostling each other in hopes of getting the best seat. "No running!" Mr. Bandorro shouted.

On a smooth surface, Stephen was as fast as a track star, but this asphalt was pitted and gravely. The other kids pulled ahead, leaving Stephen and Alex behind. Alex was disappointed that they wouldn't get good seats, but leaving his friend was not an option. Then he heard John call back from way ahead, "Good luck, Rolling Cannoli! It looks like you're not going to make it to the blimp."

Alex rushed ahead with a clenched fist, but Stephen grabbed the back of his shirt. Alex turned around and Stephen simply shook his head. Alex snapped out of it and composed himself with a few deep breaths. Then he noticed something different about his friend. Usually the picture of good-natured calm, Stephen wore an expression of angry determination.

Everyone had boarded by the time they made it to the blimp. Another teenager scanned the stamps on their hands. She was wearing a pink, long-sleeved T-shirt and a tie-dyed *hijab* that fluttered in the breeze. When she smiled, Alex almost forgot about Sophia. She looked down at Stephen and said, "My name's Ariana. Let's find a good spot."

The crew shut and sealed the doors, and the blimp lifted like a great cloud, silent and enormous. As they rose into the air, Ariana motioned to the boys to follow her.

The cabin was large with a lot of windows. But all the windows were blocked by kids pressing their faces up to the glass. Ariana walked over to John and his cronies. Alex and Stephen looked at each other in horror.

"Excuse me," Ariana said politely, tapping John on the shoulder. "You're standing in the designated handicapped area. I need you all to find another spot."

John whirled around. "Oh, yeah? Well, I need you to find your . . ." His voice trailed off as he saw Mr. Bandorro look up from his tablet. He turned to Stephen and Alex and smiled. "Game on, you little *codardos*." He stalked off with his friends.

When Alex and Stephen saw the view, they forgot all about John. The splendor of the enormous canyon surrounded them. "Wow," Stephen gasped. Alex turned to thank Ariana, but she was already heading to the front of the cabin. He caught sight of Sophia sitting with her best friend, a cute, freckled redhead named Anna. For once, she wasn't with John. Alex smiled.

The blimp landed silently and majestically inside the canyon. The students spilled out and then stopped, awed by the towering red-rock walls. Alex jogged down the handicapped ramp while Stephen whizzed by in his chair, spinning around at the bottom with a flourish.

"Let's go over there," Alex whispered. The boys edged closer to where Sophia and Anna were standing. John was only a few feet from them, but his back was turned. He was chortling with his sidekicks.

Mr. Bandorro was dividing everyone into small groups. "You four, team up." He pointed at Anna, Sophia, Stephen, and Alex.

"Uh, oh," Sophia said.

John turned around. First, Alex and Stephen had taken his turf in the blimp. Now they had taken his girl. His face turned red, and his eyes narrowed into slits of rage.

# CHAPTER 17

## *The Red Arrow*

Ariana handed out Explorer 3.0 headsets that had GPS displays. A map of the Grand Canyon outlined the course everyone was supposed to follow to Big Chimney, their destination. The hike was an ARG, an augmented reality game, kind of like the one on Stephen's computer. Holographic representations of historical events, directional cues, and other useful information would blend seamlessly with physical reality.

The part of the canyon they were going to was once considered remote, but now it was 2067; the holographic technology in the headbands allowed each team to go there alone. The Hopi people had named the area *Sipapu*, which means "the womb of the earth" because they believed it was the place where human beings first came into the world.

Mr. Bandorro jumped onto a small boulder and rattled off safety precautions. Most of the students were paying more attention to their headbands than to their teacher. As soon as he gave everybody permission to go, John stormed off, leading his group into the canyon. The less secure he felt, the louder and meaner he became. He was still spouting off about "Team Rolly Cannoli" when he disappeared around a bend.

"Stephen, may I have a word with you?" It was Mr. Bandorro. "Privately, please." Alex, Sophia, and Anna looked at Stephen, who was smiling nervously. "It's nothing to worry about," the teacher said. "It'll only take a minute."

Stephen followed Mr. Bandorro until they were out of earshot. "Stephen, are you sure you're up to this? The Grand Canyon isn't easy."

After his mom's refusal to trust him, after the abuse from John, and even after Ariana's well-meaning special treatment, Stephen lost his temper for the first time in years. "Of course, I'm up for it!" he yelled. "I got the consent form, didn't I? I didn't come all the way out here to just sit around!"

"Calm down, Stephen," Mr. Bandorro said. "Will you be putting your chair in auto mode?"

"The motor only works on even surfaces. I hardly ever use it, anyway. My arms are super strong."

"Okay. Just promise me you'll keep to the level-one trails."

"Okay, I promise!" To the side of his chair, out of Mr. Bandorro's sight, Stephen crossed his fingers. There was no way he was going to make his team stay on trails reserved for baby strollers and grandparents. "*Now* can I go?"

Mr. Bandorro nodded.

Stephen and his friends started out on a green level-one trail, but after half an hour, Anna forked the group over to a level two. No one questioned Stephen's ability, but it was harder for him to control the wheelchair on the uneven path. He kept up, but he was worried that the trail would become even more challenging. What then? John's ugly jokes rang in his ears.

Up ahead, Sophia and Alex were talking about John's rude behavior. Stephen could overhear parts of their conversation.

"John had better leave Stephen alone," Alex said.

"He's just insecure," Sophia explained. "He doesn't mean any harm. He's really a nice guy once you get to know him."

"Huh." Alex rolled his eyes.

Sophia looked over her shoulder at Stephen, who was sweating as he rolled his wheelchair up the craggy mountain path. He glanced up at her, and she averted her eyes.

She could tell that he would finish the trail no matter what. He would *not* be the weak link on the team.

They came to the first marker, a blinking green arrowhead on the ground. Alex clicked it with his foot. An image of Hopi warriors gathering equipment and putting out a campfire popped up. A woman's voice began speaking through the headsets. "Hello, I'm Dr. Mara Lightfeather. Every year for centuries, the Hopi people made the journey to their sacred site, *Sipapu*, to give thanks to Mother Earth, whom they believed could grant them good luck and good harvests for the coming year. And they began that trek right here, where you stand. Follow the trail markers. Green ones point the way. Red ones warn that you've wandered off the path and will redirect you. If you pay attention to the markers, you'll walk in the warriors' footsteps to Chimney Rock—without getting lost. Good luck!"

Dr. Lightfeather's voice went silent, and the warriors standing before the kids vanished. A track of green arrows lit up.

"Wow!" Stephen said.

"So cool!" Anna said.

Excited, they followed the arrows. Before long, they came to the second marker, a blinking green arrowhead. Sophia clicked it, and Dr. Lightfeather spoke again. "It was on this spot in 1823 that gold prospectors . . ." The kids followed along with rapt attention as their guide explained the geology of the region. Then they made their way down the Grand Canyon, choosing level one and two routes. Slowly but surely, they followed the next few markers.

They fell into a rhythm. Alex was in front, and Sophia was right behind him. Anna had fallen back to chat with Stephen. They heard the splashing of rapids, and as they came to the next twist of the trail, Alex stopped.

"Noooo way!"

When the others joined him behind a bend, they gasped. In the canyon below, the path ended abruptly. The trunk of an enormous fallen tree hung perilously between the steep, rocky banks of a river. Water rushed under the tree and through the snaking canyon. Any misstep would mean a wild plunge. Despite the danger, it was breathtakingly beautiful.

Alex was thinking there was no way Stephen could make it across the fallen tree without help. He glanced at his friend, whose eyebrows were knitted together in deep concentration.

Alex was formulating a plan when he noticed a small pile of stones by his feet. Red light emanated from within the stones. He was puzzling over this when, out of the corner of his eye, he noticed movement. He looked up to see Stephen rolling at full speed toward the river. Alex jumped, kicking over the pile of rocks and uncovering a blinking red arrowhead. Horrified, he realized that it was warning them to stay *away* from the river. They had to go in another direction.

"Stephen, stop!" Alex yelled. But it was too late. Stephen popped his wheelchair onto the log, still going full speed. In a flash, Alex realized that John's teasing had hurt Stephen's pride, making him do crazy things so he would not let his team down.

Stephen was crossing the river on his wheelchair. Alex, Sophia, and Anna stood at the bend of the trail, terrified. Despite the danger, their friend's acrobatics were impressive. With incredible balance, he rolled on a single wheel across the log. He had almost reached the opposite bank when the wheel lurched to the right. Stephen, wheelchair and all, plunged into the river.

Alex took off at a full run and Sophia ran after him.

Sensors in the wheelchair detected that it was falling, and a safety harness deployed automatically, pinning Stephen snugly in. Stephen and the chair tumbled head over heels through the rapids until the current dragged them to the bottom. The chair toppled over, and Stephen banged his head on a rock. The water roared in his ears. He struggled to unbuckle his safety harness. Maybe he could swim to the top. He fumbled with the harness again and again. He suddenly felt very sleepy. The world went dark.

# CHAPTER 18

## *In the Tiger's Paws*

Alex ran toward the river screaming, "Sophia, I need your help. Annie, call 911!"

In a full run, he dived in, Sophia plunging in after him. The water was icy cold. Alex swam well, but Sophia was on the swim team. She reached Stephen first and fumbled with his safety belt. Stephen was still. He seemed to be unconscious. Alex and Sophia had to struggle against the current to stay close to him. There was a keypad on Stephen's armrest and Alex typed in likely passwords: Taiji, Bingze, EagleWing, CaveRabbit, his fingers flying across the keypad as he held his breath. But it was no use.

"It won't unlock!"

Alex's thoughts were desperate but clear. *If I can connect with Stephen through the computer game, maybe I'll be able to get the chair's password. This time, we'll have to sync the computer ourselves! But Stephen's out cold. Maybe Sophia—*

Alex bobbed his head out of the water to take a breath. "Sophia, where are you?"

"HERE!" she screamed. Her eyes were as big as saucers, scared but brave.

"Grab my hand!" Alex yelled. They clasped hands and went under again. He had no idea if the game would count her in, but he had to try. He needed all the help he could get. The current caught Alex, and he got sucked away, but Sophia grabbed his arm and swam as hard as she could. Within seconds, they found Stephen again. Holding hands, they each grabbed one of Stephen's shoulders.

The computer was blinking, so Alex thumped it with his fist and the screen flashed back on. The words BE ALERT LIKE A TIGER glowed bright green under the water. Then the screen flicked, sputtered, and went out.

Alex panicked. Then he felt the familiar sensation of being flushed down a toilet, the screen lit, and the worlds switched.

The water was calm, warmed by sunlight. Alex was no longer holding his breath. Relieved, he looked around. He was swimming in a small pond with two other small, silvery fish. The Sophia fish was thrashing about in panic. "Alex, where are we? Are we floating or swimming? Where are my *arms*?"

"It's okay, it's okay! We're in a game!" Suddenly, a little red fish swam in front of her, swishing back and forth. "It's the only way I could think of to save Stephen."

"Alex?" Sophia was totally confused.

"Yeah! You're a fish too!"

She saw two other fish.

"Don't worry! It's only temporary!" Alex swam around Sophia in a flurry. "It's a game! See?" He soared through the water and did a loop from the top to the bottom of the pond.

"A game?" Gingerly, Sophia stretched and squirmed until she

got the hang of wiggling her tail fins. She jetted forward in the water. "*Weeeee*! This is amazing! How is it even possible? Is this real?"

"Sophia?" It was Stephen. He whizzed past her in a flurry of bubbles. "What are you doing here? How come I'm here?"

"Stephen," Alex said, "I didn't know what else to do. You fell in the water. Sophia and I dove in to help, but we don't know the password for your harness. We couldn't get you out!"

"You were unconscious," Sophia chimed in. "So how did you get in the game?"

"I was unconscious?" Stephen didn't remember falling in the water, which scared him, but then his fish-face lit up. "We can read each other's minds in the game. So, when Alex synched the computer into game mode, I guess it counted me in."

"We can read each other's minds?" Sophia said. "So, let's do it! It's hard to talk underwater."

*We need your password to get you out of your chair,* Alex explained. *What is it?*

Stephen grinned—as much as a fish can grin. *The name of my favorite feathered friend.*

*The crows!* Alex grinned back. *Which one?*

But suddenly, something changed. Sophia was the first to notice. *Uh, guys, what's that?*

Above them, the movement of something huge and orange caught their eyes. It moved closer until it broke through the watery ceiling and plunged into their midst. It was a paw.

"Swim!" Alex yelled.

The three fish darted away. Stephen and Sophia hid among the rocks at the edge of the pond. "Was that what I think it was?" Sophia gasped.

"The paw of a Siberian tiger? Yes," Stephen said.

*How do we get back?* Sophia asked. *I want to go back.*

*In all the other games, Alex and I had to apply something we learned in Tai Ji class. Once we did that, the game kicked us back into the real world.*

"Look! It's Alex!" Sophia cried.

The red fish was swimming frantically in a flurry of bubbles. Behind him, the big orange paw swooshed back and forth. Then it scooped the fish out of the water.

"Alex!" Stephen darted out of the rocks.

"Stephen, no!" Sophia screamed, but he was already swimming away. She let out an exasperated breath and went after him. They swam to the surface. Their vision was blurry, but they could make out shapes and colors—mostly a big blue and green blur.

An orange blur swept through the water, engulfing Stephen and Sophia in a soft, deadly paw.

"Stephen?" It was Alex. "Sophia? Is that you?"

"Alex! What's happening?" Sophia cried.

They were all flying through the air.

"He's *juggling* us!" Stephen screamed. "*Aaaaaghhhh!*" It was a moment before the others realized what Stephen had said and what it meant.

"But that's ridiculous!" Sophia yelled.

But Stephen was right. A Siberian tiger was standing on its hind legs in the shallow pool and juggling the three small fish. The tiger's concentration and focus were complete. His balance and control were Tai Ji *perfect*. Round and round went the fish, juggled by the tiger.

*This is what cats do,* Stephen thought. *They play with their prey before eating them.*

Alex found it hard to think straight while being tossed around in the air by a tiger. Even the most focused Tai Ji master would have had difficulty making sense of the situation, and Alex was no master. Even so, somewhere in the back of his mind, a memory drifted in. It was Dr. Bingze in one of the first Tai Ji practices Alex had gone to.

"Be in the present, Alex," Dr. Bingze had said. "Tai Ji is a meditation on being in the moment. You must relax your mind and let thoughts of the past and future drop away. Only then can you be in the here and now."

Alex clung to this memory. He let all his worries fall to the wayside. Somewhere, outside the game, Stephen was still at the bottom of the river, in terrible danger. He let the thought go. He would deal with it in time. Right now, they had a tiger to escape. He called his friends with his thoughts.

*Stephen! Sophia! On the count of three, get ready to swim!* He felt both of them agree.

*One*, Alex thought. As he went from paw to paw, he passed directly in front of the tiger's nose. *Two!* he thought. In a split second, he would pass in front of the tiger's nose again. *Three!* his mind screamed. He whipped the tiger in the nose with the hardest flick of his tail that he could muster. The cat roared in surprise, rearing back from the blow. But he stayed balanced on his hind legs and kept juggling the fish. In spite of themselves, Alex, Stephen, and Sophia had to admire the tiger's concentration and skill.

Stephen was brainstorming. *How can we make him lose focus? We need to do it, and we need to do it fast. Can we blind him somehow?*

*Let's try,* Sophia agreed. *The sun's behind him. If we can jump in front of his left shoulder at the same time, the light on our scales might blind him. Like flashing a mirror at someone.*

*It sounds simple,* Alex thought, *but how are we all going to jump to the same spot at the same time? In case you haven't noticed, we're being juggled.*

*We can do it with our synchronized brains,* Stephen replied.

The tiger's jaw opened.

"Now!" cried Sophia. All three jumped, and for a split-second, their scales flashed in the sun like a mirror.

To the tiger's utter surprise, his breakfast suddenly vanished, and a blast of light blinded him. He lost his balance, and with a surprised roar and a humongous splash, he fell into the pond.

Alex and Sophia found themselves back in the river next to an unconscious Stephen. If he was going to live, there was no time left. Alex frantically typed JACKLEEN into the computer pad. Stephen's harness stayed firmly locked. The game sputtered and glitched, making the tiger's paw appear and disappear. The computer circuits were shorting out. The enormous paw swished through the water and grazed Sophia, who had momentarily turned back into a fish. She screamed and darted away before turning back into a girl.

Alex kicked the computer, and the game shut down. He was getting out of breath, and the water was growing dim. He frantically pressed ENTER. The computer lit up, and the clasps on Stephen's harness snapped open so suddenly, Alex was knocked over. He caught a glimpse of Sophia struggling with Stephen's limp body, of legs kicking amidst the rapids. He was losing the last shred of his strength. He started breathing in water.

A woman's voice, a voice he hadn't heard for many years, whispered in his ear.

"Alex, you can't die. Kick! *Kick!*"

He kicked. He emerged blindly from the water, his hands feeling for something to grab onto. Coughing and sputtering, he heaved himself onto a flat boulder a few feet from the riverbank. As if from a great distance, he saw Sophia thumping Stephen's chest and breathing into his mouth. He saw Stephen stir and cough up water. Only then did Alex pass out.

# CHAPTER 19

## *Heroes and Villains*

Alex woke up to a terrible noise. "WHUMP, WHUMP, WHUMP." He couldn't remember where he was.

*If that's what it sounds like,* he thought, *then I'm not in heaven.* He opened his eyes. A medical helicopter was landing, sending sand and sticks everywhere. Three men in green jumpsuits got out and ran toward Stephen, carrying a gurney with them. Sophia stepped aside while they put an oxygen mask on his face and carefully maneuvered him onto the stretcher.

Alex sat up and tried to catch Stephen's eye, but he got dizzy and fainted. The next thing he knew, strong hands were rolling him onto his stomach. He coughed and spewed water onto the rock. He slowly got up on his hands and knees and heaved up more water. When he looked up, sunlight assaulted his eyes. He sat back down, feeling dizzy again.

"Stephen?"

A woman knelt next to him and handed him a steaming mug. "Drink," she said. "It's hot cocoa." She stood up and put a blanket around his shoulders. Sophia and Anna were huddled under blankets on the riverbank. They were crying. Sophia looked at him, shivering, tears running down her pale cheeks.

Alex gulped down some chocolate. "What happened to my friend? Is he okay?"

"He needs medical attention, but he'll be fine. He took in a lot of water and hit his head. He's got a big goose egg, maybe even a concussion. You kids were lucky to get out of the river when you did."

Alex sipped the cocoa. The warmth spread through his chest, returning feeling to his freezing body. He hadn't realized how cold he was.

"H-how did you know we were in trouble?"

"Your friend Annie called us on her watch-mii. You should thank her. Your other friend, Sophia, is quite the swimmer. She pulled Stephen out of the water. Those girls are heroes."

*What about me?* Alex thought. *I helped, too.*

Everybody was down on Alex, even his father, Stephen's mother, and his classmates. In the beginning, he did not expect things to go so terribly wrong. He did not want people to blame Stephen for being reckless, so he kept quiet. But then John filled up Alex's silence with his own version of events. John hadn't even been at the river, but he managed to convince everybody that Stephen's accident was Alex's fault. Stephen kept trying to explain what had happened, but nobody believed him. Stephen himself had to admit that the story sounded crazy. Rumors were circulating that Alex was going to be expelled from school.

Stephen not only had a concussion, but he also got pneumonia. He had to stay in the hospital for almost a week. When he returned to school and sat next to Alex, Mr. Bandorro asked a freckled girl named Jen to trade places with Alex, putting the two boys on opposite ends of the classroom. People were treating him like he had a contagious disease. Stephen's mother did not want him in her house.

Alone in his dark attic room, Alex kept circling back to the same problem: *why had they all taken so long to notice the arrow pointing away from the river?*

On the last day of school, there was a ceremony in the auditorium. Students got awards for perfect attendance, making the honor roll, and outstanding achievements in sports. Stephen got a robotics award. Alex gave him a high five when he came back from the stage. It was a small gold trophy shaped like a robot that waved when you pressed a button. Stephen rolled back to his place several rows in front of Alex.

"Congratulations!" Alex texted.

"Thanks," Stephen replied. "Did you see the TV crew?"

"There's a TV crew here?"

"Yeah, they're off to the side of the stage."

Alex craned his neck. Sure enough, there was a camera crew and a reporter from Channel Six News. "Must be a slow news day," Alex typed.

After what seemed like an eternity, the last award was finally given out and Mr. Skeeter, the principal, came to the podium. The camera crew shuffled around and got into position.

"Due to recent events, we have a very special award to present. It's actually new. We created it to honor exemplary students who help others in ways that go beyond the call of duty."

Mr. Skeeter cleared his throat. "During our recent trip to the Grand Canyon, some people's reckless behavior caused a serious accident. Fortunately, due to the quick action of one brave girl, it didn't end in tragedy."

Mr. Skeeter adjusted his glasses and looked at the students, who were now completely quiet. "Please welcome our Hero of the Year, Sophia Nelson!"

The auditorium went wild. People applauded and stomped their feet as Sophia made her way to the stage. Channel Six cameras rolled. Once she was standing next to him, Mr. Skeeter held up his hands in a gesture for silence.

"Sophia is not only an honor student, captain of the swim team, and president of the Science Club. She also single-handedly saved one of our students from drowning!"

A screen descended from the ceiling, and a video came on. It looked to Alex like an approaching rescue helicopter recorded it: Sophia was pulling Stephen from the river, reviving him on the bank, and standing anxiously aside to make room for the rescue workers.

"It's my honor," Mr. Skeeter said, "to present you with our brand-new Hero of the Year Award. Without your courage, the field trip would have been a tragedy. On behalf of the school, we thank you." He placed a silk ribbon dangling a gold medal around her neck.

Again, the students clapped and stomped their feet, this time chanting, "So-FEE-uh! So-FEE-uh! So-FEE-uh!"

Sophia, meanwhile, squirmed.

Stephen turned around to look at Alex. He texted, "You rescued me first."

Alex replied, "Yeah, but she pulled you out of the water."

On stage, Sophia was talking to Mr. Skeeter and vehemently shaking her head. The principal patted her on the shoulder and turned back to the microphone. She snatched it out of his hand.

"It wasn't just me," she protested. But the auditorium had gotten so rowdy, no one heard her. The chants of "So-FEE-uh" turned into shouts of "VaCAtion!"

Alex, Stephen, and Sophia made their way out of the auditorium and met in front of the school. Stephen's mother was waiting for them. "Sophia, what really happened that day? I've heard a lot of versions."

"It was all of us, Mrs. Carter," Sophia said. "Alex and I both got him out of the water, and Anna called for help."

Mrs. Carter looked at her thoughtfully. "Why don't you and Alex come over for dinner tonight? I need to hear this from all three of you."

# CHAPTER 20

## *The Other Recording*

A few days later, Sophia called Alex. "Roger wants to meet with you."

"John's Roger? What for—to make fun of me?"

"No, listen. Roger has disappeared. John's looking for him, and he's mad."

"Poor Johnny. Aren't you going to go cheer him up?"

"Alex."

"Okay, okay. Tell Roger I'll meet him in the park tonight. Nine sharp. No John, and no tricks."

"I'll tell him. Good luck, Alex." She softly added, "And be careful."

"Tomorrow I'll give you a full report," Alex spoke with as much sarcasm as he could muster.

As soon as Alex spotted Roger's bulky form on the bench, he asked, "What do you want?"

"I just want to talk. Is it safe here?"

Alex was surprised. Roger was whispering, and he looked scared.

"Safe? Are you kidding? Your boss John will protect you."

"No! He's the one I'm afraid of. After Stephen's accident, I don't want anything to do with him."

"You can't just ditch John like that. He'll cancel you."

"It doesn't matter now. You see, I'm the one who covered the red arrow with stones to direct you guys to the river. John told me to do it. We didn't expect anybody to actually try to cross the river, much less in a wheelchair! We didn't want anybody to get hurt. We just wanted to confuse you and slow you down."

"Wow. Thanks a lot."

"I'm sorry, I really am. But I can help you now." Roger pushed his greasy hair out of his eyes and looked at Alex. "There's a recording. I made it for John to prove that I did what he told me to." He fumbled with his tablet. "It's pretty short. Look."

Alex looked. The red arrow was clearly pointing away from the river. Then it was barely visible, covered with stones. Next, Stephen was crossing the log on one wheel. Then he fell in the river, and Alex ran after him, calling for Sophia to follow and for Anna to call 911. The recording ended with Alex and Sophia vanishing in the water.

He sighed. "Everybody will say this has been photoshopped."

"That's the thing," Roger said gleefully. "I have the original recording with the time and GPS coordinates. It's yours if you want it."

"Why are you doing this?"

"I've always liked Stephen. We used to talk, but then John . . . well, you know John. It was either him or Stephen. I don't know why I picked *him*. My father lost his legs in the war. He's in a wheelchair, and some days after school, I volunteer at a rehab hospital. If John knew about that, he'd call me a girl."

"There are worse things than being called a girl," Alex said.

"Yeah. Like hanging out with John." Roger got quiet, then looked at Alex with starry eyes. "The way you and Sophia got Stephen out of the river was incredible. It was impossible! Nobody can open a wheelchair like that under water." Roger was now talking fast, like he was embarrassed and had to get everything out before he lost his courage. "And the way you and Stephen handled those guys, Nitro and Weezle. That was awesome!"

"It wasn't us. It was knowing Tai Ji."

"It was both," Roger said firmly. He reached into his backpack and fished out a key. "The hospital where I volunteer? It's called St. Vincent's. I've got a locker next to the gym. The recording is there on a zip drive, whenever you want it. I would've brought it with me, but I was afraid John might follow me here." He tossed Alex the key. "I'll back you up. *I* was at the river, not John."

"Give me that, you loser!" John roared. He and his new sidekick, Tom, came charging out of the bushes in front of the bench. Without thinking, Alex threw the key as far as he could. It vanished in the darkening trees.

John and Tom stopped, not knowing what to do next. This gave Alex enough time to shout at Roger, "You take Tom and I'll take John!"

John lunged at Alex. As Alex was yelling at Roger to take Tom, he flipped John and sent him flying into the middle of a big rose bush. John screamed, "Tom, pull me out! Pull me out!" But Tom was running away with a bloody nose.

"Good job, Roger!" Alex said.

"I box every now and then."

"Let's get out of here," Alex said, grinning, "before John gets out of that bush."

"But what about the key?" Roger asked.

A glossy black crow alighted on the bench. "Hey, Jackleen," Alex whispered. "Be a good girl and bring me the key."

Roger gaped at Alex. "Are you talking to a crow? Have you gone nuts, or is this part of Tai Ji practice?"

Jackleen flew off into the trees. A few seconds later, she returned with the key in her beak and deposited it neatly on the bench. Roger's expression changed to absolute awe and admiration.

"At last, after all this training," murmured Alex, "Stephen will be proud."

# CHAPTER 21

## *The Secret of the Chinese Book*

After the school board heard Roger's confession and watched his video, things turned around. Mr. Skeeter apologized to Alex and Mr. Lasko for failing to listen to Alex's version of events, but Alex didn't get to feel like a hero. School was out, summer was coming, and Dr. Lasko was busy in Chinatown. Sophia had disappeared. John was almost kicked out of school. His grades were not good, so he had to repeat the seventh grade. He also had to do community service at a hospital for children with disabilities. Roger, in the meantime, became friends with Stephen and Alex. He also decided to learn Tai Ji.

A thunderstorm rumbled in the distance as Alex and Stephen headed to the gym for their last class before the summer break. Alex walked with his head down, his hands jammed into his pockets.

"Is something wrong?" Stephen asked.

"It's Dad. His head is always in the clouds. He promised to come to the gym for our last class, but I have no idea where he is. I wanted him to meet Dr. Bingze."

"Is that all?"

"No. I've been wanting to show him and Dr. Bingze a book, but they're both always so busy. I've got it with me now, but I don't know what to do with it. I can't just hold it during practice."

"Just put it in the hood of your sweatshirt. Nobody will notice. You can show it to Dr Bingze during the break. Let me help you." Stephen stuck the book in Alex's hood and pulled the drawstring so it would not fall out.

A golem was standing guard at the door. Alex smacked its rear as he ran past it, but the golem stood as still as a statue. It wouldn't come to life unless someone tried to interrupt the lesson by coming in late. Dr. Bingze did not tolerate lateness. He considered Tai Ji to be a meditation in motion. It was not to be interrupted, and his golem made sure no one ever forgot it.

Roger was already there. He waved when he saw Alex and Stephen come in. Stephen explained how the headsets worked, and Alex helped Roger position it. Dr. Bingze bowed and said, "Let's begin." The students pulled their virtual reality headsets down and got into position. "Standing like a tree, moving like water," Dr. Bingze said. *"Zhan zhuang, chi shui."*

Alex smiled as he went through the movements he now knew so well. He let his breath move slowly and deeply, swirling inside him until he felt it come to rest in his belly.

Suddenly, there was a noise at the front of the room. The door to the studio opened. Alex tried hard to stay focused and not turn, but of course, he turned. Everyone turned as well, curious to see who had come in late.

It was Dr. Lasko. Alex gaped at him, worried. His father did not know about the golems. He opened his mouth to say something, but just then, two massive gray arms encircled Dr. Lasko and lifted him off the ground.

The students gasped, and Alex's eyes went wide. He looked

to Dr. Bingze to help his father, but Dr. Bingze was just standing there with his arms crossed, an oddly amused look on his face.

Alex looked back at his dad. He had wriggled out of the golem's grasp and was scuttling forward. The golem tried to grab him, narrowly missing. Dr. Lasko put some distance between himself and the golem, and then he did something that astonished Alex— he assumed a Tai Ji stance.

*Dad knows Tai Ji?* Alex wondered. Many months ago, when they had gone up to the lake, his father had acted like he didn't know the first thing about it.

The golem dropped its shoulders and rushed Dr. Lasko. The class went silent. Alex tried to yell, "Watch out!" but the words stuck in his throat. The golem ran straight at his father, but just as it made contact with him, Dr. Lasko swirled his hands around the golem and stepped deftly out of the way. A Tai Ji move! The golem lost its balance and crashed to the ground.

Roger nudged Alex. "Your dad is awesome!" The class clapped and cheered, including Alex, but the smiles didn't last long. The golem pushed itself off the floor.

Dr. Lasko moved away, but the golem swiped at his foot. He tried to hop over its strafing leg, but he wasn't quick enough. He fell on his back with a thud. The golem came stomping toward him, and Alex ran to help his dad. But he tripped and fell, and the booklet flew out from his hood. It opened as it flew, as books usually do in the air. Everybody, including Dr. Bingze, froze as they watched the bizarre sight. The book grew bigger, and the pictures started to move. The golem ignored the book and moved in on Dr. Lasko. At the last moment, the picture of the woman warrior flew from the book and engaged the golem, throwing him away from Dr. Lasko.

It was then that Dr. Bingze finally said, "Stop!"

The book landed on the floor like a normal book. The golem froze, stood up straight, and faced Dr. Bingze. "Go to sleep," Dr. Bingze said. The golem trudged back to its cubby and deactivated. The lights in the cubby went out, shrouding the golem in shadow.

Dr. Bingze walked over to Dr. Lasko, who was sprawled on his back. "Hello. I'm Dr. Bingze, Alex's Tai Ji teacher." He held out his hand to help the man up.

"I'm Peter Lasko, Alex's father. He asked me to come to class."

But Dr. Bingze was mostly interested in the book. He delicately picked it up from the floor. "This is a very rare book. It really is magic. Let's finish our practice, and then we'll talk about it. Dr. Lasko, please join us." He walked over to Alex, smiled, put his hand on his shoulder, and squeezed lightly. Then he clapped hands and motioned for his students to fall into line.

Alex took a deep breath. "Everything's fine." He exhaled and engaged his *tan tien*. And with his father, his teacher, his class, and his best friend, he practiced Tai Ji.

After class, Dr. Bingze led Alex, Stephen, and Dr. Lasko into his tiny office. He picked up the book from his desk.

"I've never seen one of these before. A long time ago, my grandmother told me about an ancient family who knew the secret of magic painting. Their figures could move, even help others if needed. I thought it was just an old folk story."

"Alex, why didn't you show me this?" Dr. Lasko asked.

"Dad, I tried, but something always interrupted us."

"It's true, Dr. Lasko," Stephen chimed in. "We were talking about the book when we went fishing and swimming."

Dr. Lasko rubbed his chin. "Well, yes, now I remember . . ."

"My grandmother told me," Dr. Bingze went on, "that magic books like this were used as messages."

"Messages?" Dr. Lasko was suddenly alert.

"Yes. Why? Are you expecting one? From China?"

"It's impossible," Dr. Lasko murmured.

Dr. Bingze cocked his head to one side. "What's impossible?"

"I've been waiting for the last six years for a message from my wife, Alex's mother."

"Well, let's look for it." Dr. Bingze carefully thumbed through the pages. "It's usually just a date and a place. The story of Princess Ling comes from the Nanjing area, where there's a famous mountain with a huge boulder. And the flying crane . . . hmmm. I wonder if it means the airport."

"The Nanjing airport!" Excited, Alex looked at his father.

"Your mother told me I would have to fight a monster before I could receive her message. It didn't make any sense—until now."

"The golem!" Alex and Stephen gasped.

"If I hadn't fought the golem, and if that character hadn't jumped off the page to help me, I wouldn't believe any of this." Dr. Lasko looked at Dr. Bingze. "And without you, we would never guess the meaning."

But Dr. Bingze was already thinking about the date. "Here—this flower—it only blooms once a year, and only for a day." He studied the Chinese calendar hanging by the door, looked at his watch, and studied the calendar again.

"When?" Alex breathlessly asked.

"I don't know." Dr. Bingze sighed. "Maybe we can Google it."

Dr. Lasko, who had been peering at the illustration, slapped his forehead. "Stupid me! It's *fuscalia fuscalia barbarica*, a medicinal herb. I should have recognized it right away."

"*When*, Dad? When does it bloom?"

"Same time every year—the day of the new moon in July."

Dr. Bingze squinted at the wall calendar. "That's the ninth this year."

"Dad, today's the fifth!"

"Oh my God, we've got to go to China! Now!"

Alex was a ball of emotions and racing thoughts. His mother, the mother he barely remembered, might be in danger. They had to find her. He would have to leave Stephen and Sophia. Would he ever see them again? What would his mother be like? Why had she left? What had she been doing all this time?

Dr. Bingze looked at the book again. "Yes, you must leave as soon as possible. But be careful: the monkey playing with boulders means a lot of adventures!"

# CHAPTER 22

## *The Great Magic Crane*

The very next day, Alex and his father packed their things. In the living room, Dr. Lasko reached behind the white cover over the sofa. He pulled a large picture and put it on the mantle above the fireplace. It was a painting of a Chinese noblewoman in a rich, traditional brocade dress. The man and the boy looked at her in silence. At last, Alex said firmly, "We'll find you, Princess." Peter Lasko couldn't say anything; he was suddenly fighting something wet in his throat. Alex also felt like crying. His father was suddenly in such a hurry; he had to say goodbye to his friends over the phone.

"But you'll be back, won't you?" Stephen had asked.

"Yes, but I don't know when. It could take years to find my mom."

"Let's all pray to St. Anthony," Sophia said. "He helps you find lost things."

They walked out of the Brooklyn townhouse. Dr. Lasko closed and locked the door behind them. Alex stood on the curb and looked up at the empty building that had been his home for the past few months. Leaving would be bittersweet. Hopefully, they would find his mother, but he was going to miss his attic room and the crazy energy of the city and most of all, his friends. Especially Stephen, the wheelchair kid he'd gone on so many adventures with, and Sophia, a girl who turned out to be as brave as she was pretty. An auto-cab hummed to a stop in front of them. The doors hissed open. Alex and his father put their bags in the trunk. They climbed in, and Alex yanked the strap to close the door.

"To JFK Airport!" Dr. Lasko said. The lights inside the cabin blinked green for a moment and then the auto-cab hummed toward its destination. It crossed an intersection, and Lincoln Park opened up around them. Alex was daydreaming, as usual, his thoughts in China, when his father said, pretending to be surprised, "Is that who I think it is?"

Alex looked out the window and gasped. On a bench in the middle of the park, he spotted Sophia. Seated next to her in his chair was Stephen, throwing seeds to the birds. There were a few crows among them, and Alex wondered if Stephen's crows were waiting for him there.

Alex yelled, "Cab, stop!" The vehicle pulled up next to the park. Dr. Lasko smiled, his eyes twinkling. "Go say goodbye to your friends."

Alex threw the door open and ran like crazy across the tall grass. Stephen and Sophia looked like they were expecting him. Alex spread his arms wide, and they hugged.

"I wish you two could go to China with me," Alex said as they broke the hug. At that moment, Stephen's computer screen lit up with the words THE GREAT CRANE SPREADS ITS WINGS.

The three friends synced.

Alex was falling fast into darkness. Wind wailed as he plummeted down. Then the darkness evaporated, as fast as rain on hot cement. The space became lit by the sun. Alex was tumbling through the air, out of control, high above a lush landscape. He glimpsed a majestic mountain, then a valley, then a stream flowing through the valley. A boulder teetered on the edge of the mountain. A mischievous monkey was screeching and dancing on the enormous stone. The boulder rocked back and forth.

Alex knew where he was. He was inside the book he had found, the book his father was probably studying while he waited in the auto-cab. In a moment, that enormous stone would roll down the mountain, the tiger would roar a warning, and the panda would save the little tree. Next, the crane would turn the tree back into Princess Ling. Where *was* the crane? Alex could not see it anywhere.

As he struggled to get control of his body, the world stopped spinning and merely tilted from side to side. *Now I'm getting somewhere,* he thought.

He rolled to the side again, but this time, he felt like he was in one of those dreams when you desperately want to move but can't. "*Agh!*" he shouted, but instead of his voice, he heard the throaty squawk of a bird.

It took a moment, but he finally grasped the gravity of the situation. *Hot Helga! I'm the Crane! I am the one who's going to save the Princess—if I can get control of myself and don't smash into the ground.*

He heard Stephen and Sophia gasp. He wondered where they were. He couldn't see any other cranes anywhere near him.

*Where are you two?* Alex thought.

*I don't know! I can't tell,* Sophia replied.

*Me neither,* Stephen said, *but I'm starting to wonder if I'm part of a bird.*

*Weird,* thought Alex as he tried to steady himself. Had the game malfunctioned? *Can either of you move? Stephen, try waving your arms around.*

They were coming down fast. Alex was about thirty seconds away from becoming a crane pancake. This wasn't how he wanted to say goodbye to his friends. He tried with all his might to flap his wings, to right himself in the air, but he was paralyzed. Except for his head, he couldn't move a muscle.

*Is it working?* Stephen's voice echoed in Alex's rattled brain.

*What?* Alex could barely think.

Then he remembered that he had just asked Stephen to wave his arms around. "Stephen, stop!" He quickly regained his senses. Sophia and Stephen weren't stuck in a glitch of the game. They weren't separate cranes, either. Together, all three of them were the *same* crane.

*I can see now!* Sophia said.

*Me too!* Stephen chimed in.

"Listen up!" Alex screamed, but he cut himself short. He had momentarily forgotten that, when they were in the game, they could read each other's minds. *A lesson: in Tai Ji, the body has to move in one harmonious whole, like a team working together. We're each in charge of one part of the crane!*

*I'm the best swimmer,* Sophia reasoned. *So, I must be the legs.*

*Alex is the fastest,* Stephen thought, *so he's the wings.*

*And Stephen's the smartest,* Alex finished. *He's the head! Guys, we can do this! Take charge of your part, or we're done for!*

The three friends tried with all their might, but the crane kept falling. "Hot Helga!" Alex yelled. "This is just the opposite of how I wanted to say goodbye."

*That's it!* Sophia thought. *It's the opposite. Our weaknesses are our strengths. I have weak arms. I'm the wings! Stephen's the legs! Alex is hyper and squirmy. He's the head!*

Her words flashed through the boys' brains.

"Hurry, or we'll die," Alex screamed. "Fly up! FLY UP! We have to turn the tree back into a princess!" Stephen tucked the bird's legs under, Sophia flapped the wings, and the great white crane soared into the sky, barely missing the ground.

The monkey screeched and jumped as the boulder went crashing down the mountain. The tiger roared. The panda leapt in front of the boulder. The crane swooped in and made three graceful circles over the little spruce.

"*Yoopie!*" They all celebrated the triumph. Alex bobbed the crane's head in a wacky dance. "We can fly, we can fly, oh, we don't have to try, oh me, oh my, gonna eat a pizza pie!" he squawked.

"You're such a goober!" Sophia teased.

"That's not all we can do," Stephen said. "Look!" A graceful young woman stood where the tree had been only a moment before.

"She's so beautiful," Sophia whispered.

Princess Ling's horse emerged from a glade, snorting his greeting. The princess smiled. "Daoji! I'm so glad you waited for me." She stroked his face and he snorted again. "I have nothing to give you, but when we arrive at the palace, you'll have all the carrots you can eat."

Princess Ling mounted Daoji, and the horse carried her away.

"I hope King Ka has forgotten about her," Alex murmured.

"Who's King Ka?" Sophia asked.

"A character in the story we're inside," Alex said. "Hey guys," he added, "we need to leave the game."

"But we're just now having fun," Sophia said. They had left the mountains and valley behind and were now flying over the open sea. The water sparkled in the sunlight. A pod of dolphins danced in the waves. An emerald island beckoned not far ahead.

Somehow, the crane was losing its strength. It glided toward the ocean. *I have to find my mom,* Alex reminded them.

*Of course. I just hate to see you go.* Sophia sounded sad, even while thinking.

*We have to figure out the lesson to get back,* Stephen reminded them.

*Maybe it's that there's strength in weakness,* Sophia suggested.

*My legs don't work,* Stephen agreed, *but my weakness has forced me to get better at other things.*

*That's not it. The crane is getting weaker and weaker.* Alex's mind began to shout. *We're going to drown! Maybe, this time, this game is looking for our hidden weaknesses.*

*Not the obvious ones,* Stephen thought, *like our arms and legs and head.* His voice became more tender and soft than he wanted it to be. *Alex, do you mean a weakness like me being afraid of making friends because of my voice and wheelchair?*

*Or like me caring more about being popular than being myself?* Sophia sighed deeply, like a person throwing away a heavy load.

*That's my weakness, too, plus I need to control my temper,* Alex confessed. *But my biggest one is weird. With my dad and me constantly moving, my mom somewhere in China, and my dad always so preoccupied, I have no idea who I am and where I'm going in life.*

*That's deep, Alex. Very philosophical,* Sophia murmured. *I like it.*

Stephen's computer screen flashed: I LIKE IT TOO!

The three friends would never know if it was Stephen's thought or the computer's, but the falling crane disappeared. Lights flashed, then it got dark, then light again, and they were back in Lincoln Park.

"Alex!" Dr. Lasko was calling from the auto-cab. "We have a plane to catch."

"I have to go." Alex hugged his friends goodbye. "Don't forget me!"

"Alex, this has been the best year of my life! I'll never forget you, my friend," Stephen said. "Eagle Wing bros?" He stuck out his fist. Alex tapped Stephen's fist with his own.

Stephen opened his hand. "This is for you. I found it in the pants I was wearing in the canyon. It's for luck."

"Thank you." Alex took the gift. It was a smooth, polished pebble from the bottom of the river in the Grand Canyon. It fit perfectly in his hand. "Thank you," he said again, trying not to cry.

Feeling awkward, he turned to Sophia.

"I want to hear all about China." She smiled. "Email me, and I'll email you back."

Impulsively, Alex leaned over and kissed her on the cheek. "Bye, guys!" Waving, he ran back to the auto-cab. The crows, startled and offended, flew into the sky above the park. Alex still couldn't tell which one was Jack and which one was Jackie. But he knew Jackleen, the master of keys. And without a doubt, he knew he would see Stephen and Sophia again.

*The end.*

Far away in the tall Jade Mountains, there lived a beautiful princess named Ling. Princess Ling roamed the forests and valleys on her horse, but she never hunted the animals. Instead, she painted them in the most magical way; they looked so alive, people swore they could see them move across the page.

The cruel King Ka wanted to marry Princess Ling, but she did not love him, so she refused his proposal and ran away. King Ka sent his soldiers to capture her. They rode swift horses and caught up with her at the foot of the White Dragon Mountain.

The Great Crane, a good magician, was flying by. He saw what was happening, so to save the princess from the evil king, he turned her into a little spruce tree. The animals loved Ling and protected her. She grew straight and proud by a tumbling stream. Her roots spread into the earth, and she got taller and taller, as if reaching for the sky.

One spring morning, a monkey was playing with the boulder on the top of the mountain. He danced and pushed until it tipped over. Down it flew, gathering speed as it went.

The tiger, always alert, saw the danger and roared. The panda bear lunged. He bent under the great weight of the boulder, pushed it aside, and saved the princess.

Just then, the Great Crane flew over the mountain. King Ka had married the mean Princess Boo, so Great Crane knew it was now safe to turn the little spruce back into a princess.

# *Acknowledgments*

Hey, we are kids at heart. Without that, we couldn't have written this book, so we are thankful to our parents and grandparents. Also, we are grateful to our wives, two wonderful women who have supported us, edited our work, and made us more resilient to the writer's lot. Thank you, Linda Voychehovski and Sophia Prater! Other magnificent friends involved in this treacherous process were Carol White, Eleanor Cooper, Tom Kunesh, Lenny Rubin, and Sheila Rubin. Special thanks also go to the Chattanooga Tai Ji Community, the Socrates Café, and our writer's groups. And last but not least, to John Koehler for bringing this project to book form, to Miranda Dillon for her close editing, and to Danielle Koehler for her beautiful cover design. Cheers to all!

Printed in the USA
CPSIA information can be obtained
at www.ICGtesting.com
LVHW010234201123
764406LV00029B/474